Shane Brown was born in 1974 and lives in Norwich, UK. He received a doctorate in Film, Television and Media from the University of East Anglia in 2014.

He is the author of the horror novels *The Successor*, *The Pied Piper*, and *The School Bell*, as well as the young adult novels *Breaking Point, Breaking Down*, and *A Ghost of a Chance*. Shane has also written books detailing the careers of Elvis Presley and Bobby Darin.

Follow the author on Twitter @shanebrown74.

Copyright © 2021, by Shane Brown

Front Cover:
Snow at Argenteuil by Claude Monet

GHOST STORIES FOR CHRISTMAS

Shane Brown

CONTENTS

Houses Never Forget   11

The Philatelist   37

Breaking Up is Hard to Do   73

The Stranger in the Snow   95

The Gift   123

A Note from the Author   137

HOUSES NEVER FORGET

Every village has one: a house that is supposed to be haunted, or, at the very least, that kids think is haunted. Brandley was no different.

The school was about a mile from where I lived and I would walk it every day, firstly with my mother, and then, after about the age of seven or eight (I really can't remember precisely), I would go alone.

About mid-way between the school and my home was the main village shop, which was, perhaps, bigger than most village shops. Back then, it was called Mace, then it went to Happy Shopper, and then on to Spar. The names changed with regularity, but the shop itself didn't really alter, other than an occasional reorganisation. But the sweets and chocolates remained in the same place. That was all us kids were interested in.

I'd also pass the small doctor's surgery on my way to and from school, and there was a hairdresser's called The Beauty Parlour which, looking at the hair-dos of some of the people who went there, must have been a name given for the purposes of irony.

But, beyond these few commercial premises, the main street of Brandley was made up of houses. Mostly old cottages. There was an occasional new house, but not many. This was, after all, thirty-five years ago, before developers started buying up land to create sizeable new housing estates that would eventually double the population of the village. A number of the old cottages had names on the gates, or on the front door. I remember that one was called Orchard Cottage, another was Primrose Cottage. There was also Treetops, and, at the end of the road on which I lived, stood The Hollies. None of the names were anything remarkable. Most villages probably had their own homes with names that were similar or the same.

But the one that I remember most was The Gables. I didn't really notice it when I was still walking to and from school with my mother, but, once I started doing the journey alone, passing it twice each day became a moment of dread for me.

There was nothing particularly remarkable about The Gables. It was a decent-sized cottage dating from the early-Victorian era. The exact year was given on the date stone, a few feet above the front door. 1847 was the date. Like most things about The Gables, I would never forget it. The front garden was mostly given over to a lawn, and there were various flowers planted around it, although the garden as a whole could have done with some care and attention. There were five windows at the front of the house. There was one each side of the front door – presumably for what in the old days would have been viewed as a living room and a drawing room. On the next floor were three more windows, which I always assumed were for bedrooms.

It was the window to the left of the front door that I will never forget. One day, when I was about eight or so, I went past the house and looked towards that window, and on the sill was a skull. I had no idea whether it was real or not, but I no doubt thought that it was. At that point, I wasn't frightened by the sight of it, but was more curious. Even at that age, I was wondering why someone would want that on their windowsill. Every day afterwards, I would prepare myself as I approached The Gables. I didn't want to look at the skull in the window, but, for some reason, I couldn't help but look across to see if it was still there or not.

I must have mentioned the skull to a friend at school (not that I had many) because the other kids started talking about it, and rumours started spreading that The Gables was haunted. There seemed to be no reason for this, other than the fact that the skull was in the window, and I felt that I was somehow responsible for the reputation that the house was getting. After all, it was I who had first commented on it.

But, as the rumours spread, I dreaded walking past

the house more and more. What had always looked like a pleasant cottage now seemed to take on a more sinister feel. It was almost as if the whole personality of the house had changed – as if the house had actually become haunted since the kids at school had started talking about it that way. It got to the stage where I would stop walking a little way from the house, pull myself together and then run past it as quickly as I possibly could. I was pretty sure that I wasn't the only one who did so.

This went on for several months, until one day, when I started running past the house, the front door opened, and an elderly man stepped out on to the footpath in front of me. There was a car coming, and so I couldn't run around him. I had to stop right in front of the house.

The man was probably in his late seventies or early eighties. He was bent over, and used a stick to help him walk. There was a cap on his bald head, and a pair of glasses perched on the end of his nose. He stood in front of me on purpose, and put his hand on my shoulder.

"So, it's you, is it?" he rasped at me.

I didn't really know what to say, and so I quietly confirmed that it was me.

"You don't realise," he snarled. "Houses never forget when you wrong them."

He smiled at me – a smile that I could only see as evil at that age – and then walked slowly past me.

I was shaking by this point. I was scared for all kinds of reasons. Firstly, I had been stopped outside of the house that I dreaded passing so much. The man himself seemed menacing, something like a villain from a Roald Dahl novel. And then there was what he had said. "Houses never forget." What did he mean by that? Deep down, I think I was aware that he had probably said it just to frighten me. Perhaps he had seen me running past the house each day – but then, the thought of him secretly watching me from behind one of the net-curtained top floor windows was also a scary one.

If I had been thinking straight, I no doubt would have started running again. But, instead, I turned towards the house. It was the first time that I had seen that window for months. I had always run past it. I wished I hadn't looked, for the skull was no longer sitting with the side of its head along the window. Instead, it was staring straight at me, and the eyes seemed to be glowing. I took one look and ran as fast as I could – not just past the house, but all the way home.

The next morning on my way to school, I felt that I had to stop and look at that window, just to make sure that I hadn't been seeing things. And there it was. The skull was facing me, and those eyes were glowing again. I told my friend at school of the latest development, about how the position of the skull had altered, and how the eyes glowed with a kind of white light. He told me that it hadn't been like that when *he* had come past. And this made it even more frightening – and made me the butt of jokes at school for the rest of the week. I was now obsessed with the idea that the house somehow felt wronged by me for having inadvertently started rumours that it was haunted.

I never looked in the window again. Time went on, and I ran past the house each time I had to pass it. And then, eventually, there was the move to high school, which involved catching a bus each day, and I had very few reasons to pass The Gables after that. I grew older, and ultimately memories faded about the house that had frightened me so much as a kid.

I went away to university when I was eighteen. I met a girl while I was there, and we set up home together after we had finished our studies. We got married, had kids, and were separated by the time I was forty. By this point, I was a headteacher at a primary school near where we had made our home together. I needed a fresh start, and I had the idea of moving back to Norfolk. I started looking for jobs, and, after a few weeks, I saw that the position of headmaster at Brandley Primary School had become vacant. It seemed almost like fate that I could end up as headmaster at the school I had myself attended between the ages of four and eleven. I applied and got the job.

Returning to the village in which I grew up was, perhaps, a little disorientating to start with. My parents had since moved about ten miles away, and so I hadn't had any reason to return to Brandley in many years. I found myself a home in one of the new housing estates that had attached themselves to the village in recent years. It was a characterless place to live, and wouldn't have been my first choice, but I had to find somewhere quickly and at the right price. There was always the option of selling the house in a few years' time and then moving to somewhere that was a little more to my liking.

The school hadn't changed a great deal, other than having had a couple of extensions built on to it since my time there as a pupil. These extensions were, of course, to accommodate the extra children that the housing estates had brought to the village. There was one teacher who had taught me as a nine-year-old who was, miraculously, still teaching there, but she said she didn't remember me, and for that I was oddly thankful.

The autumn term passed with little incident. I got to know the staff, and they got to know me. I got friendly with a few of them, but not too friendly. I knew from my previous position that a headteacher who grew too close to the other teachers was likely to run into difficulties if and when they did something they needed to be talked to about. Nevertheless, on the final day of term, a young teacher knocked on my office door and asked me if I would like to join him and his wife (Elise, apparently also a teacher at the school) for a drink that night. He said that they would be at The Swan pub at eight o'clock. I was welcome to join them, I was told, and I said that I would.

The truth is that I had to ask someone who the teacher was. Clearly, he was one of those who had quietly gone about his business and had not said anything at staff meetings. Even so, I felt it was a little weird that I didn't recognise him. And none of my colleagues were able to decide who he might have been from my description. Three people gave me three different possible names, and none of them turned out to be correct.

I arrived at the pub a little after the appointed hour, and joined the couple at the table they were sitting at. The Swan was the village pub. It had been The Lamb's Head when I had lived there in my younger years, although I had never worked out why pubs were invariably named after animals (or, indeed, parts of animals).

Through some rather careful prodding on my part, I found out that the couple's name was Gerald and Elise Matthews. It seemed to me that Gerald seemed a very old name for a young man. Who called their kids Gerald these days? But I thought little more of it.

"So," Gerald said, after we had got our drinks, "how has the first term been?"

"Uneventful, thankfully," I answered. "It's nice to have had a term of relative tranquillity before any drama starts."

"Yes," Gerald said. "But there isn't often much drama in a place like Brandley. There were the ups and downs of Covid at the school last year, of course. The school was quite badly hit by it. And you know, of course, that one of the teachers, Melanie Bird, died from the virus. It was very sad, really. She was a much-loved teacher."

"Yes, I did know," I said, although I had been told by a parent rather than any of the teachers. "She was relatively young, I think someone said."

"Fifty-ish. Mad as a hatter, if you ask me. But the

kids thought the world of her, and I shouldn't speak ill of the dead."

"That's the second time that phrase has popped up this week," Elise said, sipping at her wine. "One of my reception class came out with it a few days ago. A very strange thing for a five-year-old to say. It gave me the creeps, actually."

"Sometimes, they just hear a phrase on the telly and pick it up for some reason," I said.

"I suppose so," Elise said, somewhat vaguely. "What was your last school like?"

"Not much different to this one, in all honesty. I only left because I separated from my wife, and I thought a new start would do me some good."

"So, what are you up to over Christmas?" Gerald asked me.

"Not much," I said, honestly. "My parents live locally, but they had already promised to go to my aunt's to stay this Christmas. It was arranged before I got the job here. I have been asked if I want to go, but I said no. I'm not really one for going away at Christmas. I like to be able to do what I want, when I want, rather than be awfully polite in the house of a relative I barely know."

"Then you must come to us," Gerald said. "Mustn't he, Elise?"

"Yes," Elise said. "You must."

"Thank you for the offer," I said. "But I couldn't possibly intrude on you on Christmas Day."

"Then how about Christmas Eve? Come around

and have some drinks. There's only us two."

I paused for a moment. I didn't really feel like being sociable, but saw no way out without upsetting Gerald and Elise.

"Thank you," I said. "Where do you live?"

I cannot express the feeling of dread that came over me as soon as I had asked that question. I knew instinctively what the answer was going to be.

"We're on the main street," Gerald told me. "A cottage called The Gables. You probably remember it from when you lived here as a child."

★

I should have made some excuse not to go to Gerald and Elise's house on Christmas Eve. I could have told them I was ill, or that I had gone with my parents to stay at my aunt's after all. And yet, for some reason, I didn't.

I spent the days after the evening at the pub thinking of little else other than The Gables. It totally dominated my time. If I sat down to read or to watch a movie, my mind would quickly switch off from whatever it should have been doing in order to think about that cottage.

I found that I was unable to sleep. It didn't matter what time that I got to bed, as soon as I closed my eyes, I would see that skull in the window, its eyes glowing. I tried taking sleeping tablets, but they did little good. They got me off to sleep quickly, but, an hour or so later, I would wake up from a nightmare, and that would be the end of my sleep for the night. I managed to catch up a little by sleeping during the afternoon, but, even then, I was only dozing.

The strange thing was that I hadn't really thought about The Gables since my return to Brandley. It was only after that night at The Swan. I wondered if my mind had somehow blocked out my experiences as a child, and they had only resurfaced with a vengeance after I became aware of the fact that I was to actually go there for an evening. The odd thing was that I hadn't even driven past the place since I had moved back to the area. I lived at the other end of the village, and there was no real reason for me to drive through the main street.

But I wasn't a young boy anymore. I shouldn't have been scared by the prospect of going into a house that I had inadvertently helped to give a reputation of being haunted. In fact, I should have been genuinely curious to see inside the old place at last, and to lay my childhood demons to rest. After all, many people go to visit haunted houses and other locations for fun. But the thing that scared me wasn't really that skull in the window, but the man who had come out of the cottage when I was a child and told me that "houses never forget." Those words somehow gave the house a personality, it made it seem like a living thing with a conscience and a brain. I wondered how many other kids he had scared over the years, and also what had happened to him. I assumed that Gerald and Elise were not related to him in any way.

Eventually, Christmas Eve arrived. The various

last-minute bits and pieces for Christmas had been done. The cards I had forgotten to write had now been written and delivered. The final trip to the supermarket had taken place. And I was, rather strangely, looking forward to seeing absolutely nobody on the big day. I planned to get up at lunchtime, open presents, cook myself some lunch (not a Christmas dinner, too much hassle for one person), and then get steadily pissed during the evening while watching whatever film was on the television, which I assumed would be either *Harry Potter* or *James Bond*, as they seemed to be the mainstay of bank holiday programming these days. Gone (for better or worse) were the days of *The Wizard of Oz*, *The Great Escape*, and *The Sound of Music*.

All I had to do to have this day of relative luxury was to get through a couple of hours at The Gables. It was about a mile away from my own house, and I decided it would be best if I walked there, as it would allow me to drink without worrying about staying within the legal limit for driving.

No snow was forecast, and so it wasn't going to be a white Christmas in the traditional sense, but it was bitterly cold, and certainly a white frost would be covering the roofs, cars, and gardens when the world woke up on Christmas Day. I was rather glad that it was so cold. At least it made me think about how cold I was instead of what horrors I might face when I arrived at my destination. Of course, I was being silly thinking that there might be horrors. It was just a house, and it had a very pleasant, friendly couple living in it.

About twenty minutes after setting out, I arrived at The Gables. It was the first time I could ever recall being outside of the house without running past it. There was no skull in the window, and, instead, there were Christmas lights around each of the windows on the ground floor. There were more around the front door. It looked welcoming, but so do all the cottages in the fairy tales we get told as children – and they are invariably inhabited by witches.

I took a deep breath and walked up to the front door, and rang the bell. A couple of seconds later, the door was opened by Gerald, who was wearing a suitably naff Christmas jumper, and had a glass of wine in his hand.

"Come in!" he said, a big grin across his face.

I took another deep breath, knowing there was no turning back now. I smiled back at Gerald, and went inside.

"Let me take your coat," Gerald said, closing the door behind me.

I took off my gloves and shoved them in my coat pocket before handing it to him. Then, I pulled off my shoes and left them near the front door.

"You must be freezing," Gerald said.

I was, but the cottage was warm, bordering on hot – or perhaps it was just the cold outside that made it feel like that.

"Yes," I said. "There's a good frost out there. It might well be icy in the morning."

"Come through into the lounge."

GHOST STORIES FOR CHRISTMAS

I followed Gerald through into the lounge. The room where I had seen the skull when I was younger. It wasn't there now. Instead, the room was very welcoming. There was a log fire on the go, and Elise was curled up on a chair, wearing a thick woollen jumper.

"Hi," she said. "Glad you could make it. Sit down, you'll soon warm up in here."

I thanked her, and sat down on the sofa. Gerald asked me what I would like to drink. I settled on a brandy. He brought one over to me, and then brought various bowls and plates of snacks in from the kitchen and placed them on the coffee table.

"Help yourself," Gerald said, and I reached out and took a sausage roll, which was still hot from having been in the oven.

"Not home-made, I'm afraid," Elise said.

"They're nice," I told her.

"What are you up to tomorrow?" Gerald asked, sitting down on the sofa beside me.

"Nothing," I said. "Absolutely nothing. I'm going to have a quiet day on my own. I'm rather looking forward to it, actually."

"There's just us two here, too," Elise said. "Until the evening, at least. The next-door neighbours have invited us around in the evening. So, we will get quietly pissed there."

"I don't blame you," I said.

"Have you been inside here before?" Gerald asked. "Most people in the village seem to know the house by reputation, but haven't ever been inside. The previous owners never had many friends, from what I can gather."

"What do you mean by it having a reputation?" I asked.

"Oh, I thought you'd know all about it, having lived here when you were younger. It has a reputation of being haunted. But the previous owners said that they had never experienced anything of that sort while they lived here, and I even searched to see if anything bad had happened here – you know, murders etc. Nothing. And we haven't had anything happen to us, have we Elise?"

"No," Elise said, while pouring herself another glass of wine. "Nothing's happened to us. Quite disappointing, really. I like the idea of living in a haunted house."

"I think every village has one, don't you?" Gerald said to me. "A house that's reputed to be haunted, or an old woman who is believed to be a witch. That kind of thing. Probably some kids started the rumours decades ago, don't you think?"

I nodded.

"Yes, probably."

"And you know what it's like," Gerald went on. "Houses never forget."

My stomach churned as I heard the words.

"What did you say?" I stammered.

"I said that such rumours never really die out. They never get forgotten."

Was that really what he had said? That rumours

don't get forgotten? I was certain that it wasn't. Perhaps my mind was playing tricks on me. Maybe I'd had one too many drinks during the afternoon, and on an empty stomach, too. I was surely imagining things.

"Are you alright?" Gerald said to me. "Brandy too strong?"

I forced a smile and gestured to my glass.

"No, not at all," I said, taking a mouthful. "You're right. These places get reputations, and they stick for some reason or other."

"Yes. We did a bit of digging at the library before we bought the place, though. Just to make sure that it didn't have a horrible history of some kind, didn't we, Elise?"

"Yes," she said. "We found nothing that might give it a reputation."

"Nothing at all," Gerald confirmed. "Do you remember things being said about it when you lived here before?"

I shook my head.

"No, not that I recall," I lied. "But it was a long time ago, of course."

Gerald exchanged looks with Elise, and I wondered if they knew that I was not telling the truth. I became uneasy at the thought that there might be something going on between them that I didn't know about. I had no idea as to what it could be. They were far too young to know about the kind of things that were said when I was a kid. And yet I felt as if I was being played in some way.

"It's odd, though," Gerald was saying. "Most of the kids all stay away at Halloween. They never come here to trick or treat. We watched them this year, didn't we, Elise?"

"Yes, we did."

"They went to all the houses on the other side of the road, and then crossed over and went to the house next door, and then they ran past ours as fast as they possibly could before going to the neighbours on the other side. It was almost as if they felt there was someone or something about to pounce on them. Oooohhh!"

He made the supposed sound of a ghost while wiggling his fingers in the air. Then he looked across at Elise, and she did the same. And then they did it together. It was bizarre, and oddly grotesque.

"And then there's the teenagers," Gerald said. "They inevitably tend to play pranks. The little devils."

"Another drink?" Elise asked. "Get him another drink, Gerald."

I felt as if I should refuse; that I should make some excuse to be on my way. The evening was beginning to have a slightly surreal feel, but I tried to convince myself that it was only being caused by the alcohol. Even so, all I really wanted to do was go home. Something inside of me told me to get out of that house.

"Have something else to eat," Elise said, as if she was reading my mind. "It will help soak up the alcohol. It will make you feel better."

"Thanks," I said, quietly, and helped myself to a

handful of crisps, eating them quickly, one after the other, in an attempt to hide my increasing nervousness.

"Perhaps you should show him around the house," Elise said. "Go on, Gerald, take him on a little tour."

Gerald smiled at me. A forced smile if ever there was one.

"Would you like to see the rest of the house?" he asked me.

"Yes, that would be nice," I said.

The lounge seemed to be getting hotter by the minute – or was it just my own anxiety making me think that way? Either way, I was keen to get out of the room.

Gerald got up from his seat and went to the door, and I followed him. As we went out into the hallway, I felt that I could smell something burning. It wasn't the log fire in the lounge; this was a different smell.

"Can you smell something burning?" I asked Gerald, as he led me into the dining room.

He turned his head and sniffed in the air with a great deal of exaggeration.

"No, I can't smell anything. Perhaps it's Elise's cooking? Those sausage rolls were a little overdone. Not that I'd tell her, of course!"

He winked at me, but something didn't feel right. Everything about the evening had begun to feel wrong. I couldn't put my finger on it exactly, but it was what I can only describe as a gut feeling.

"Well, this is the dining room," Gerald said. "It's rather a nice room, I think. It was a second reception room when the place was built. A drawing room, I guess they'd have called it."

"Yes," I said, trying to concentrate on what he was telling me.

"And there's this rather nice date stone above the fireplace. Not that we use the fire in here anymore. 1846. A different date to the stone over the front door, which is a bit odd."

The initials H. N. F. were inscribed beneath the date. I asked Gerald if he knew what the initials stood for.

"No. We were going to try to find out, but we never got around to it. Perhaps we will one day. Come through into the kitchen."

As we left the dining room, I realised what the initials could possibly stand for:

Houses Never Forget.

But that was a stupid idea. It was no doubt the name of the builder or maybe the designer of the building. And yet, I couldn't put it out of my mind. All of these strange happenings over the previous half an hour or so were beginning to go around and around in my brain, and I was beginning to feel as if, somehow, I wasn't in control of what was happening.

The kitchen was surprisingly large for a cottage of that size, and everything within it seemed strangely old-fashioned. I assumed that the retro design of the cooker and fridge-freezer was intentional, probably to try and fit in with the cottage itself as much as possible. On the draining board were some items of crockery, all of which also seemed from a slightly different era.

"All the mod cons," Gerald said. "We only just got the fridge-freezer. Got it on H.P. at Rumbelows."

"Rumbelows?"

I knew that they had disappeared from the high street years before. Gerald looked at me as if I was going mad.

"Rumbelows?" he asked me. "What's Rumbelows?"

"That's where you said you had got your fridge."

"No. Currys. You must have misheard me. We got it at Currys on Black Friday. Half price, it was. Quite the bargain."

"Yes," I stammered. "It sounds it."

"I'll take you upstairs," Gerald said, and led me back into the hallway and up the stairs.

Despite being out of the lounge, the house seemed to be getting hotter. I put my hand on a radiator as we reached the top of the stairs, and found it to be stone cold. So, where was the heat coming from?

Gerald led me into the first of the bedrooms. It was decorated as a nursery. There was SuperTed wallpaper on the walls, and a cot in the corner.

"I guess this is giving the game away," Gerald said. "But Elise is…well, she's having a baby. Quite a while to go yet, of course, and she's hiding it pretty well. But you'll need to find someone to cover her during her maternity leave. Hope it won't be too much of a problem for you. But we're very happy. We've been trying for ages."

I smiled and congratulated him.

"That's wonderful news," I said. "I'm very pleased for you."

Then he took me into the main bedroom. Again, I was struck by how old-fashioned the decoration was, and I suddenly remembered that I hadn't seen SuperTed on the television for years. Had it been remade recently? I hadn't heard anything about it – not that I would be the target audience, of course, and it seemed that nearly every old series had been "rebooted" recently.

"The house is looking wonderful," I said, almost on autopilot by this point, just wanting to get through the rest of the evening and then get home.

"Thanks. It's taken us a little while to get it how we want it, of course. Now, come back down and have another drink."

"Can I use your bathroom first?" I asked.

"Of course."

Gerald showed me the bathroom door, and then went downstairs. I quickly went into the bathroom and locked the door. I staggered over to the bath and sat down on the side of it, trying to make sense of what was going on. Part of me just wanted to go downstairs and run out of the house, and never come back. But I was the headteacher, and what would Gerald and Elise say about me at the school if I did something like that? I didn't want the teachers thinking I had lost my mind.

The heat in the house seemed to be getting worse, and so I went over to the sink and turned on the cold tap, splashing the water on my face to try to cool myself down. I realised that I was sweating, and my shirt was sticking to my back. I took it off, and used the water to wash and cool down my body. As I dried myself with the towel, I realised just how ill I was feeling. The sick feeling was no doubt partly due to the heat and partly due to panic. Something was wrong, and I needed to get out of there.

I looked at myself in the mirror above the sink. I looked terrible, and, as I ran my fingers through my now-wet hair, I noticed that my hands were shaking. Putting my shirt back on, I looked once again into the mirror, but the face that stared back at me was not mine. It was the face of the man who I had met coming out of the house when I was a boy. There was no mistaking it. That face was one that I had never forgotten, and that had haunted me in nightmares even in my adult years.

"Houses never forget," he mouthed, although he made no sound, and then he grinned, showing off his chipped and blackened teeth. And then the smile gave way to a laugh, a laugh that didn't just come from the mirror, but from the entire bathroom. No, the entire house. The structure of it trembled with the volume, and I had seen and heard enough. I had no idea whether I was being the victim of some horrendous practical joke or whether I was losing my mind – and I didn't care if I was going to be the laughing stock of the school when it returned after the Christmas break. My main aim was to get out of there.

I unlocked the bathroom door and ran down the stairs as fast as I could. The front door was already open, and I ran through it onto the street and across the road, feeling some degree of protection from the houses on that side of the street.

When I turned to look back at The Gables, I saw that it was not there. The house I had entered had gone, and it had been replaced by a property that couldn't have been more than about ten or fifteen years old. What was more, I realised that I was wearing my coat and shoes, both of which should still have been in the house I had just left, for I had not stopped to put them on when I had escaped.

I wanted to run home, but I couldn't. I felt dizzy and disorientated. It was difficult to walk, and the journey that had taken me just twenty minutes earlier in the evening must have taken me an hour to complete on the way home. I stumbled into my own house and almost fell onto the sofa. My exhaustion must have taken over at that moment, for I woke up on Christmas morning, just as the sun was coming up. I got up off the sofa and walked over to the window, where I opened the curtains to reveal a bright and crisp, frosty morning.

*

On Boxing Day, I got the courage to get into my car and drive along Brandley's main street. I wanted to see The Gables – or whatever was in its place – in the daylight. I was confused and frightened. What had happened to me, and what had happened to Gerald and Elise?

When I drove past on that morning, I saw that it was, indeed, replaced by a modern building. The Gables was gone.

When I returned to the school in the first days of the new year, I found out that there were no teachers at my school named Gerald and Elise. No wonder why I hadn't recognised them. But how was that possible? It was almost as if I had dreamt the entire thing. When my secretary came in, I asked her if she recognised the names.

"There was a young couple teaching here with those names when I started as secretary," she said. "But that was a long time ago."

"What were they like?" I asked.

"I don't really remember. I was only here for a term or so before they…"

"Before they what?"

"Well, before they died. There was a house on the main street, an old cottage it was. Quite well-known among the villagers. It had quite a reputation – the kids made out it was haunted. The man who had owned it – I don't know his name – had passed away, and this couple, Gerald and Elise, had bought it when they moved to the area to start work here.

"But the man who had lived there before, he had rubbed the kids up the wrong way, you know? They used to go there and stare at the house to see if they could see the ghosts, and he'd chase them off. And so, the children started playing tricks on him. Mostly knocking on his front door and running off. Getting him covered in flour on Halloween when they were trick or treating. That kind of thing. Horrible, but not dangerous.

"But when he died, the kids didn't stop their pranks, even when the new couple moved in. I suppose they took it in their stride. I'm not even sure some of the kids realised the old man had passed away. Some probably didn't. But one of the pranks got out of hand. It was on Christmas Eve, and a couple of lighted fireworks were shoved through the letterbox. The place caught fire. It had to be pulled down."

I listened to the story in horror. If I hadn't told my friend about the skull in the window, then the cottage wouldn't have got a reputation as a haunted house, and those pranks would never have happened.

"What happened to the couple of teachers who lived there?" I asked. "Did they die in the fire?"

"Oh, yes. A great shame. A nice couple they seemed to me, from what little I had seen of them. They were expecting a baby, too, from what I remember. But that only came out afterwards. That's the problem with kids starting rumours and saying things that aren't true. They don't realise the consequences there might be further down the road."

THE PHILATELIST

Joshua Hale was an ugly baby. Whereas most mothers were used to people coming up to them and complimenting on their beautiful baby, nobody did that to Mrs. Hale when she was pushing Joshua around in his pram. Most often, when someone peered into the pram, they smiled weakly and then made an excuse to go on their way quickly.

As he grew into a toddler, his looks improved somewhat (they couldn't get much worse), but his behaviour became a problem. He would scream his way around a supermarket, purposefully knocking over the various displays. Joshua was also very good at running off down the road, often into oncoming traffic. He would also swear at anybody who passed him on the street, although the Hales had no idea where he had learned such language from. Mr. and Mrs. Hale were, after all, weekly churchgoers, and would never use such language themselves – well, not where anyone could hear them, at least.

By the time he started school, Joshua had acquired something of a reputation. In lessons, he showed himself to be remarkably bright, but his behaviour had not improved, and he often made life difficult for his teachers, who secretly hoped that his family would suddenly need to move from the area. That didn't happen.

Shortly after his fifth birthday, his mother sat him down in the living room and asked him what he would say to the idea of having a little brother or sister. Joshua said quite bluntly that he didn't want one. This was not the required answer, and so his mother said that he was getting one anyway, and that it would arrive in about six months.

"I wish him good luck," Joshua said, and then got up off the chair to play with his Lego.

When Mrs. Hale told Mr. Hale of this development, Mr. Hale said that Joshua would get used to the idea, and everything would be fine. But Mrs. Hale was not as hopeful.

"I don't know what to do with him," she told one of the other mothers when she waited for Joshua to come out of school one day. "He can be something of a devil, you know."

The mother she was talking to smiled and said, "no, I'm sure that's not true" while thinking completely the opposite. Most people who knew Joshua didn't think that he was *a* devil, they thought he was *the* devil. In all of the village of Brandley, nobody could remember a child as disliked as Joshua – if "disliked" was the right word. "Feared" would perhaps have been more apt.

On Christmas Day, 1970, Mrs. Hale gave birth to her second child. Isaac, unlike Joshua, was one of the most beautiful babies that any of the nurses at the hospital had ever seen. From the outset, he seemed to be the complete opposite of Joshua. He rarely cried as a baby, and from the very beginning would refrain from waking up his parents during the night. As he grew up, Mr. and Mrs. Hale knew that they could take him anywhere and he would be perfectly behaved. At the school where teachers had fought not to have Joshua in their classes, the same teachers all wanted Isaac. If Joshua was a devil, then Isaac was a saint. He seemed to have a calming influence on all of the children that he came into contact with.

Except Joshua.

Nobody and nothing had a calming influence on Joshua.

By the time that Isaac started school, Joshua was ten years old, and the problems kept coming for his parents. They were told at a parent's evening that Joshua had a "mouth like a sewer" and would often swear at the teachers. He had thrown a stone at one of them during playtime, and hit the teacher in question on the head. A few centimetres lower, and it would have taken out an eye.

"We just don't know what to do with him," Mrs.

GHOST STORIES FOR CHRISTMAS

Hale told the teacher.

"Think how we feel," the teacher replied, with no attempt at humour. "The problem is that he is a very bright child. If he wasn't, he wouldn't get away with half of the things that he does. He has taken to doing lewd drawings on my blackboard, but I have never caught him."

"What kind of lewd drawings?" Mr. Hale asked.

The teacher squirmed in her seat.

"Well," she said, "normally bums and penises." She mouthed both "bums" and "penises" without making any sound, as if she would be struck down by lightning if she said the words out loud.

"How do you know they are done by our son?" Mr. Hale asked.

"Who else would it be?" came the reply.

Mr. and Mrs. Hale couldn't argue with that reasoning. They tried to chastise Joshua, but he said that he was innocent of all charges.

Things went from bad to worse when Joshua made the move to high school the following year. With alarming regularity, his parents would get a call from the school, telling them of the latest horror he had got himself into. He had a particularly cruel streak, ideal for the bullying of others. While he made the life of certain kids absolute hell, he did so without any physical force, and it was therefore more difficult for him to be severely punished. The headteacher at the school was keen to suspend or expel him (just to get rid of him), but knew he had no grounds for doing so. Joshua even escaped detention most of the time, simply because teachers didn't want to have to spend more time with him than they absolutely had to. The less they saw of him, the better it was.

There were times when Joshua *did* find himself in serious trouble. This included the time he brought a penknife into school and threatened to carve his name into a boy's chest with it. There was also the time when he smoked outside the school gates and pushed the lighted cigarette into the arm of a girl who had pushed him away when he had tried to kiss her.

Meanwhile, Isaac continued to be the model pupil through primary school. He might not have been quite as clever as his brother, but he was still good at his work, and none of the teachers ever had to raise their voice at him. His teachers tended to feel sorry for him, and wondered how horrible it must be to have to live with Joshua.

When Isaac was eleven, he went to stay with his grandparents, who lived on the coast, during the summer holidays. Joshua was not invited to join him. In fact, his grandparents did their best to stay away from him as much as possible. They had come to stay with Joshua and his parents one Christmas, and found it so traumatic that they never came again – at any time of year.

And so, that summer, Isaac was put on a train by his parents with the belief that the break from Joshua would do him good. After all, by the time Isaac went on that trip, Joshua was making his life hell. If Isaac bought a record with his pocket money, Joshua would ask to borrow it and then make scratches all over it. If Isaac was reading a book, Joshua would take it when he wasn't looking, and rip out the last chapter. When Isaac got a new bicycle for his birthday, Joshua scratched the paint on one side. Joshua was a dab hand at scratching paintwork on all kinds of vehicles – including police cars and the vicar's Vauxhall Viva.

Isaac didn't know his grandparents well, but he bonded with them very quickly. In fact, he decided that he would very much like to live with them all of the time, but his parents were not willing for that to happen. But Isaac and his grandparents spent much time on the beach, and they took him on various trips to local places of interest. And they spoilt him a great deal.

One day, Isaac's grandfather was attending to his stamp collection when Isaac walked into the room.

"What are you doing?" he asked.

"This is my stamp collection," he was told. "They are stamps from all over the world. Some of them are very old."

"Why do you collect them?"

"Because I find them interesting. I always have done. Ever since I was a boy about your age. There are all the designs, and all the different countries they are from – many of which no longer exist. And sometimes – but not very often – you find that one of your stamps is worth a great deal of money."

"How much?"

His grandfather told him.

"Think what you could do with all of that money," he said.

Isaac pondered for a moment.

"I would buy a house and move away from Joshua," he said.

"That's not very nice."

"Neither is Joshua."

Isaac's grandfather did not argue this point.

"Perhaps we should start you off on your own stamp collection," he said, instead. "Would you like that?"

Isaac said that he would.

"Good. We'll visit the stamp shop tomorrow or the next day, and see what we can find for you."

By the time Isaac returned home to his parents and brother, he had a stamp album, a guidebook to collecting stamps, and a starter pack of two hundred stamps. When he got off the train, he proudly told his parents that he was now a philatelist.

Mr. and Mrs. Hale were happy to have Isaac back home, as he had something of a peaceful effect on the house. But they no longer knew quite what to do with Joshua. They knew he only had one more year of compulsory schooling, and they were worried as to what would happen afterwards. How long would it be before he started taking drugs? Or worse, selling them? How long before he got himself in to trouble with the police? And, heaven forbid, how long until he got a girl pregnant? If truth be told, they were surprised it hadn't happened already.

Joshua spent his last year of school by mostly avoiding the place altogether. His parents were aware that he was leaving the house with his schoolbag and then going somewhere else entirely. It was, perhaps, for the best that they didn't know the exact location. The school rang them repeatedly to inform them that their son was not in attendance. Mr. and Mrs. Hale often spoke to Joshua about this to start with, and then they eventually gave up, knowing that their talks were doing no good. Joshua no longer took them seriously, if he ever had. When his schooling ended, he continued to spend his time doing nothing except causing trouble and annoyance to other people.

Isaac remained a model pupil. His teachers adored him, even if his brother didn't. His fellow pupils were indifferent. They saw Isaac as something of a swot, but didn't make his life difficult, and many had sympathy for the way he was treated by his brother, both at home and on the few days when Joshua turned up at school.

Life might not have been easy for Isaac, but he did get a great deal of enjoyment out of stamp collecting, something he now spent almost all of his pocket money on. His grandparents often sent him interesting specimens for his collection, and he went to spend time with them as often as he could. Joshua would not have wanted to go with him, but he was still annoyed that an invitation wasn't extended to him each time Isaac went away.

Joshua soon began to realise that stamps gave Isaac a great deal of pleasure, and he became jealous. He

THE PHILATELIST

desperately wanted to ruin Isaac's enjoyment, but was at a loss at how to do it. He was tempted from time to time just to steal his albums and the box of unsorted stamps, but he knew he didn't really have the nerve – and he was also aware that it would ultimately do little good, as his parents would simply do their best to make up for the loss. He wouldn't put it past them to make him leave home if he sabotaged Isaac's hobby, and that would mean getting a job to pay rent somewhere, and he had absolutely no interest in doing that.

But, to Isaac, the stamp collecting was turning into something more than just a hobby. He took a part-time job at the weekends, and used the money he earned to extend his collection. Over time, he managed to track down some valuable items, and added them to it. He was beginning to see his collection as a way out of living at home with his brother.

One evening, a couple of weeks after Isaac's eighteenth birthday, he found himself at home alone with Joshua on one of the occasions when their parents had gone out. Joshua spent most of the evening sprawled out on the sofa, a can of beer in his hand and several empty cans on the floor. When he got up to use the bathroom, he passed Isaac's room. He stopped to look in through the open door, and saw that Isaac was sitting at his desk with the stamps in front of him. Joshua walked over to the desk, bent down and blew the loose stamps on the floor. Isaac turned to him.

"What did you do that for?" he said.

Joshua grinned.

"What are you going to do about it?" he said.

Isaac scowled and started picking up the stamps from the floor.

"I don't know what you see in them," Joshua said. "Little tiny bits of paper."

Isaac got up off his chair and stared at his brother.

"They are my ticket out of here," he said. "Away from *you.*"

Joshua's grin faded. He wasn't used to Isaac answering him back. Up until now, Isaac had always avoided confrontation.

"What do you mean?" Joshua asked him.

"What I mean is that I'm going to university. Away from you. Away from Mum and Dad."

"You know they haven't got the money for you to go with."

"*I* have the money," Isaac said. "I have the money because I've worked."

"Your stupid little job at the shop is going to take you to university? Yeah, right."

"No," Isaac told him. "I'm going to sell my stamps, and *they'll* pay for me to go to university."

"You love your stamps. You'd never sell them."

"You'd be surprised what I'd do to get away from you."

Joshua stared at him, and realised that Isaac was serious. He was both proud and angry. He was proud that it was his tormenting of his brother that was driving him out of the house. But, at the same time, he was angered that Isaac, five years his junior, was going to be the first of them to move out of their parents' home. Joshua knew that he would have to do something to stop that from happening.

What's more, Isaac needed bringing down a peg or two. He had never talked to Joshua in that way before, and Joshua didn't like it. He had bullied his brother for eighteen years, and he certainly wasn't going to let him rebel after all of that time. He needed to be taught a lesson.

But Isaac's life had changed in ways that Joshua was not aware of. Through his part-time work at the local shop, Isaac had met a colleague by the name of Will. Their work schedule meant that they saw a lot of each other, and they had become firm friends very quickly. Isaac hadn't really had a close friend before, even during all of his time at school. He had never been willing to let anybody in, and his difficult relationship with his brother hadn't helped with regards to giving him confidence to make friends. But Will was different.

The shop was often quiet in the evenings when they were working together, and they talked a great deal. Will had opened up about how his relationship with his father was difficult and sometimes abusive. Isaac then said the same about his brother. A couple of nights later, when they had locked up the shop and were about to start the walk home, they kissed.

Isaac had never really thought about sexuality. He was eighteen, and had never really been interested in girls, but he hadn't realised that it was because he *was* interested in boys. Before Will, there had never been any hope that he might get in a relationship with anyone. Will had changed everything.

In the days and weeks after, they had talked about how they wanted to escape from their family home. Both said that they wanted to go to university, and the two young men decided that they would both apply to the same one. They applied without their parents ever knowing, and both had received offers. Finally, the future looked brighter, and his oncoming escape from Joshua and his burgeoning relationship with Will had given Isaac the confidence to stand up against his brother even further.

Joshua, meanwhile, knew that something about his brother had changed, but he couldn't work out what it was. He wondered if he might have got a girlfriend, but realised that such a thing was close to impossible. So, why was Isaac suddenly standing up to him? He didn't like it, and he wasn't happy about it.

A couple of weeks went by.

Joshua's parents had got into the habit of going down the local pub once a week in order to watch the darts matches. Occasionally, Mrs. Hale was called upon to stand in when a player was ill. She wasn't a great player, but she could hold her own. Joshua was also out of the house on the same night of the week. Isaac had no idea what his brother and his friends did every Wednesday night, and he didn't really care. He was more than happy to have the house to himself for three hours or so once a week.

And so it was that Isaac asked Will if he wanted to

come over.

Isaac and Will had not yet been inside each other's houses. Neither of them had any interest in introducing the other to their family. Besides, too many lies would have to be told. No-one knew that they were boyfriends, or, indeed, anything other than colleagues at work. Homosexuality wasn't spoken about in the village of Brandley in 1988, except in hushed tones about an old man who lived on the main street and that everyone assumed was "one of them." He wasn't, as it happened, but a trivial thing such as the truth was unimportant once rumours started.

Will knocked on the door of Isaac's house about fifteen minutes after Mr. and Mrs. Hale had left for the pub. Isaac answered the front door and ushered Will into the house quickly, in the hope that the neighbours wouldn't see that he had a visitor. He didn't want them asking him who his friend was the next day. Isaac slammed the front door shut, put his arms around Will, and kissed him.

"Are you sure your parents aren't going to come back and catch us?" Will asked, as they stumbled into the living room.

"Positive. They'll be back at about eleven o'clock."

"And what about your brother?"

"He won't be back until the early hours of the morning. He never is. He's probably robbing somewhere."

The last comment was meant as a joke, but Isaac had often wondered just where his brother got his money from.

Isaac and Will ran up the stairs and into Isaac's bedroom.

"This is where all the action happens then, is it?" Will asked, smiling.

"It's where all the action is *going* to happen," Isaac replied.

"Are you sure you want to do this?"

"Yes," Isaac said. "Are you?"

Will nodded.

"I think so."

Isaac kissed Will again and they flopped down onto the bed. A few minutes later, they were close to naked.

"Now what happens?" Isaac asked.

"I thought you were the expert?" Will said, teasing him.

"I haven't a clue what we're doing."

"Me, neither. Does it matter?"

Will got up and knelt beside Isaac, pulling down his boyfriend's underwear as he did so.

It was at that moment that the pair of them heard the front door open. Isaac knew by the amount of noise being made that it was Joshua.

"You need to hide," he said, panicking. "Get under the bed."

Will got on the floor and slid under the bed. Isaac put Will's clothes on the floor so that he could pull them under the bed also. Then Isaac pulled the covers over himself, just as Joshua opened the door of the bedroom.

"You're in bed?" Joshua said. "At half past eight?

Caught you wanking, did I?"

Isaac slumped on the pillow, trying to do his best acting.

"No, I'm coming down with something. Just wanted to go to bed."

"There's nothing wrong with you, Isaac. You're a lousy liar. You must think I'm stupid."

Isaac didn't comment on that suggestion. Joshua walked over to the bed, grabbed at the covers and pulled them off. Isaac tried to protect his modesty with his hands.

"You don't sleep naked," Joshua said, throwing the covers back at him. "So, something's going on here. I can smell it."

He looked around the room, trying to work out what was going on, and then walked to the door and turned around to face Isaac.

"I'll find out what's going…"

As soon as Joshua stopped speaking, Isaac knew that he had seen Will under the bed. Joshua walked to the end of the bed, got on the floor and looked underneath.

"Coo-eee," he said, before pulling Will out from under the bed.

"Well, well. What have we here?" he said. "Two naked blokes in one room. One of them hiding. What could that possibly mean? I knew something was going on, Isaac. You should never have stood up to me the other week. You gave away the fact that something had changed in your pathetic life. And now I see it's even more pathetic than I thought."

Joshua looked at Isaac and then said to Will:

"I don't know who you are. But if I see you here again, I will bloody kill you. Now get out."

Will looked across at Isaac, and then bent down to get his clothes.

"I said get out, not get dressed. Go!"

Will ran out of the room, and, moments later, the front door slammed.

"Now," Joshua said, turning to Isaac. "What are we going to do with *you*, my dearest queer brother? You're not perfect after all, are you?"

Joshua was bright enough to know that harming Isaac physically would do him no good at all, but he hadn't forgotten the fact that Isaac had told him that some of his stamps were valuable. He had been trying to work out how he could use that to his advantage, and now the answer had fallen straight into his lap.

"Those stamps of yours," Joshua said. "How much are they worth? Quite a bit, I would imagine, if they were going to get you to university for three years. Notice how I used the past tense there. I think we can come to a much better use for those stamps now, don't you? How about you get me one hundred pounds by the end of the week, or I'll start telling people about your little secret? You've got enough stamps to get that amount quite quickly, I would imagine."

Joshua turned and walked out of the door.

"This is going to be fun!" he called, from the hallway.

Isaac quickly got dressed and went over to his desk

and sat down. He had no idea how he was going to deal with what had happened. Getting Joshua the money he wanted wasn't going to be difficult; a number of his stamps were worth one hundred pounds of more, although he had kept that information mostly to himself. The only person who knew was his grandfather, and Isaac knew that he wouldn't be passing on the information to Joshua. The biggest problem was therefore not going to be paying his brother now, but how to stop him blackmailing Isaac in the future.

Whereas his future had looked bright just an hour ago, now he felt an impending sense of doom, and he knew the only way out of it was to tell his parents that he was gay. But that was not a straightforward thing to do. Joshua had always been viewed as the wayward son, as the one that caused problems. Isaac was the one they were always proud of, the one they looked to in order to bring calm upon what was often a troubled household. He wasn't sure that he could let them down in order to save his own skin.

In the short term, Isaac didn't have to worry about selling off part of his stamp collection. He had enough cash saved up to give Joshua the money he wanted. When he handed it to him a couple of days later, he told Joshua that was all he was going to get, and if he tried to extort more money from him, then he would simply tell his parents the truth.

"You're not going to do that," Joshua said.

"And why not?"

"You wouldn't want to tell them that their favourite

son is a fairy. Can you imagine the looks on their faces?"

"I'm leaving anyway to go to university, and so it will be no big deal," Isaac told him.

"You don't believe that any more than I do."

That wasn't strictly true. Isaac had come to the decision that, after the initial surprise, his parents probably would take the news well, even if they would worry about him.

"I'll take my chances," he said.

"And what about your little boyfriend?" Joshua said, grinning. "How would *his* parents take the news?"

"Leave him out of this!"

"I don't think it's me bringing him into it. How much would you pay for *his* parents not to know? They're quite the churchgoers, too, from what I hear. What would they do? Chuck him out of the house? How would you feel about that?"

Part of Isaac didn't think that his brother would say anything to Will's parents. He didn't know them anyway, so what was he going to do? Just turn up on their doorstep and give them the news? Write them a letter? That was hardly Joshua's strong point. Even so, he thought that Joshua would find some way of telling them if he really wanted to. There was only one way forward.

The following Sunday, all four of the Hale household sat at the dining table for the weekly roast dinner. It was the one time a week when Joshua actually ate with the rest of the family. When Mrs. Hale, always the last to finish, put the last forkful of roast potato in her mouth, Isaac took a deep breath, and said:

"I'm gay. I wasn't going to tell you, but someone has found out, and I didn't want you to hear it from somebody other than me."

There was a silence for a few seconds, and then Mrs. Hale reached over and put her hand on Isaac's.

"We know, dear," she said. "We've known for some time."

"Times are changing," Mr. Hale said. "It's not such a big deal anymore. You're still our son, and we love you."

Joshua stood up.

"I don't believe this," he shouted. "He's queer and you don't give a shit. As soon as I do something wrong…"

"Being gay isn't doing something wrong, Joshua," Mr. Hale said.

When Isaac retreated into his bedroom, he felt relieved. Joshua no longer had a hold over him. Telling his parents the truth had been the right thing to do, and it had taken away all of Joshua's power. But it marked a turning point in the relationship between the two brothers. Joshua's hatred for his brother turned to sheer malice. He wanted to hurt Isaac – badly.

Joshua had always known not to harm Isaac physically, because the bruises (or broken bones, if he had his way) would make it too obvious. Now, though, he no longer cared. And he knew that even the mere threat of physical harm would make Isaac and Will's lives miserable. Meanwhile, he took to trashing Isaac's room. Isaac had come home from sixth form to find his pillow slashed to pieces. Another time, he went into his bedroom to see his radio-cassette player broken on the floor, and the aerial on top of his portable television was broken in half.

Isaac knew that it would only be a matter of time before Joshua got to the stamps. He wasn't sure whether Joshua would steal them and try to sell them, or whether he would simply ruin them. He had visions of Isaac setting light to them. But Isaac could not think of anywhere that he could hide them where Joshua wouldn't find them.

A month later, Joshua leaned against the school gates, waiting for Isaac to come out of sixth form. Joshua's behaviour was beginning to have consequences. He owed money – to the wrong people. He intended to get money out of Isaac, even if he had to beat it out of him.

When he came out of the school building, Isaac saw Joshua, and quickly ran off to leave through a different gate, but he wasn't quick enough. Joshua had seen him, and soon got to the other gate to catch him there.

"What do you want?" Isaac asked him, as they started walking home.

"Do I need a reason to meet you out of school?"

"I'm not six," Isaac said. "I can walk home by myself. So, what do you want? More money?"

"How did you guess?"

"Because you always need money, and you always seem to come to me for it. I'm not your personal bank,

Joshua. If you've got yourself in the shit, sort it out yourself."

"I know that you can do that for me."

"I can, but I won't."

"Oh, but I think you're wrong."

"Really? Think again."

Joshua pushed Isaac up against a street lamp.

"You'll do what I say, or you'll never see a single one of your precious stamps again," he said.

"What have you done with them?"

"Nothing. Yet. Just put them somewhere safe where you'll never find them."

"And what good will that do you? You don't know which ones are valuable and which ones aren't."

"I'll find out."

"I doubt that. Take the stamps, and see how far they'll get you."

"You'll do as I say."

"No. Those days are over, Joshua."

Joshua punched his brother in the face, and blood started to pour from Isaac's nose.

"You bastard!" Isaac shouted at him.

"I can do much worse than that."

"Then do it. I'm not giving you anything, you little shit!"

It was then that Joshua really came after him. He knew that Isaac wouldn't give him the money, but at least giving his brother a beating would leave him with a sense of satisfaction. By the time he had finished, Isaac's face was a bloodied mess. His left eye was swollen shut, and blood poured from his nose and his mouth, which had two less teeth than it had had half an hour before.

Joshua walked off down the street, leaving Isaac on the grass. He turned around to see him trying to stand up, but failing. He hadn't got the money, but he had the stamps in the hiding place he had found for them. He would sell them, even if he didn't get the full value of them.

He had walked about fifty metres down the road when he heard the squeal of brakes and a woman screaming. Joshua knew instantly what had happened. The realisation just hit him hard in the stomach. He turned around and started walking back down the road. Isaac was lying in the street, and he wasn't moving.

★

Christmas Day, 2020. Joshua Hale sat alone in the living room of what had been his parents' house. It was the first time in three decades that he had been back in the home he had grown up in.

On the day that Isaac had died after being hit by the car, Joshua had come home, packed a bag and left. The intervening years had not been kind to him. There had been three prison sentences, four wives, and a beating at the hands of drug dealers that had relieved him of many of his teeth and the sight in his right eye. His mother had died ten years earlier, following a stroke. But he hadn't even returned home on account of that. Now,

THE PHILATELIST

his father was dead, too, and the house that Joshua hadn't set foot in for over thirty years was legally his. His homecoming had turned out to be as miserable as the rest of his life. But at least he now had somewhere to live – or sell.

The house was depressing. Most of it hadn't been decorated since he had left. The woodchip wallpaper he had remembered was still on the walls. It had been painted over a couple of times, but it had begun to peel away from the wall. The carpets looked the same as the ones that had been on the floor thirty years earlier, although he doubted that was actually the case. His parents had simply replaced the old carpet with one that was virtually the same.

And now, on Christmas morning, Joshua was sitting in what had been his father's chair, a tumbler full of whisky in his hand. He looked like his father. What hair he had left was combed over on top, and his face was weathered and wrinkled. He looked considerably older than his fifty-five years. Joshua hadn't put on weight in his middle-age. He would have looked better if he had. Instead, his body was almost bird-like, scrawny, like a malnourished seventy-year-old.

Joshua drank the rest of the whisky, and then got up to pour himself another one. He didn't know what he should be doing. What was he to do on his own on Christmas Day in his childhood home? It was not just that it was Christmas Day, either. It was also what would have been Isaac's fiftieth birthday. Perhaps he should have been kinder to him. The smart-arsed, goody-goody loser. But if Isaac had still been alive, Joshua wouldn't have got his hands on the house at all.

The room was depressing. There were no Christmas decorations, and no cards on the mantelpiece; Joshua had received none. He had not spent the previous three decades making friends, and most of his family thought he was dead – or, at least, that he ought to be.

Joshua sat down again, and pointed the remote control at the television, flicking through the channels. Christmas Day, and nothing for him to watch – unless he wanted James Bond, Harry Potter, repeats of *Only Fools and Horses* or a Christmas service from some cathedral or other. They all looked the same to him. He settled on a Hallmark movie. Quite why he settled on that movie, he couldn't say. He was hardly a fan of bland romantic comedies with actors and actresses that nobody had heard of. But the lead actress was pretty. He watched it for ten minutes or so, and was about to get up for another refill of his whiskey glass when the scene changed to a boy in his bedroom. The boy was sticking stamps into an album.

Stamps.

Joshua hadn't thought about stamps for a very long while. His mind was beginning to whir with the amount of alcohol he had consumed, but he remembered that Isaac had a stamp collection. It had been worth a decent amount of money at the time. Isaac was going to sell the stamps and use the money to go to university. And Joshua had hidden them up. He wondered if they were still there, all these years later. Perhaps his parents had found them. He put his glass down on the coffee table, and went across the room, bending down by a grating in the corner. Joshua had never worked out why it was there in the first place, but it had been a good place to hide the box of stamps. He sat down on the floor and tried to peer in, but it was too dark in there to see anything. He took out his mobile phone, and switched on the torch, shining it into the grating. Yes, there was definitely something in there. He pulled at the grating to try and remove it, but it refused to budge.

Joshua got up off the floor and stumbled through into the hallway and out of the back door. His dad's tools were probably still in the shed. There would be a screwdriver there. The shed was unlocked, and he went inside, brushing aside the cobwebs as he did so. Clearly his father hadn't used the place much in his final years. There was a toolbox on a bench, and Joshua soon found what he wanted. He went back inside the house and set to work on removing the four screws that held the grille in place. It took a bit of time to loosen them, but eventually they budged.

Joshua put his hand inside the cavity and tried to reach the box that was in there. A spider crawled over his hand, and he withdrew it quickly. Beatings he could deal with, but spiders he could not. He shone the torch back into the hole, but couldn't see any spiders – not even a cobweb. Perhaps it hadn't been a spider after all. He slowly put his hand back inside, and made contact with the box. He pulled it out quickly and it fell onto the floor.

There it sat in front of him. "ISAAC'S STAMPS. KEEP OUT" was written on the front in thick black pen. Joshua looked at it, strangely unsure if he wanted to open it. He started to realise that, if it wasn't for the stamps, his brother would still be alive. Joshua had done many things in his lifetime, most of which he felt no remorse for, but the death of his brother was something he had not fully come to terms with. That was on him. It was why he had left home and never came back. He hadn't even telephoned his parents or written. They had effectively lost two sons that day.

Joshua swept the dust and cobwebs from the box, and then wondered why he had felt compelled to exhume it from the space in the wall. After all, he didn't need the money that it could create now. He had the house. He could sell it, pay off his debts, and disappear and start afresh. And yet something had made him want to look at it. That kid in the film on the television. If he hadn't had the film on, then he never would have remembered the stamps.

He slowly lifted the lid off the box. Inside were various small envelopes, each one had a different country's name written on it. Joshua flicked through, and realised that the envelopes appeared to be in no particular order. He pulled out one that was labelled "Portugal" and tipped the contents on to the coffee table. To Joshua, the stamps looked dull and boring. There was nothing of interest to him there, and he wondered how anything so banal as a stamp could be worth money.

He put the stamps back in the envelope, and took out another. This one read "Mauritius." There were only three stamps in this one. At least they were more appealing than those in the previous envelope. The first one had a king's head on it. The second had a flag of some sort. He dropped the third, but when he went to pick it up, he saw that it was bright red. When he touched it, he realised that it was wet. The stamp, and his fingers, were covered in blood. He yelled out in surprise and let the stamp fall from his hand. When he looked down at it, he saw that it was just an ordinary stamp, neither red nor bloody. He shook his head, thinking that the early morning whisky was making him see things. That must have been what it was. What else could it have been? He scooped up the stamps, put them back in the envelope, and put the envelope back inside the box. Then, he put the lid on quickly, and pushed it away from him.

He'd had too much to drink. That was all it was. He needed something to eat. Something to soak up the alcohol in his stomach. Joshua got up off the floor and staggered into the kitchen. There was hardly a stack of food waiting to be eaten. He must have been the only person at Christmas not to have cupboards and the fridge full to capacity. He found a packet of crisps, and opened them quickly, surprised that his hands were shaking. He took a handful of crisps and stuffed them into his mouth. As he went back into the living room, he saw the box of stamps on the floor. He picked them up, went outside and dumped them into the wheelie bin. That was the end of them.

Stuffing more crisps into his mouth, he decided he would try to get some sleep. He had arrived late the previous night, and could do with some time in bed. He walked up the stairs, past the bathroom, past what had been Isaac's room, and into the small room that had been in his own. Joshua wondered why his parents hadn't sold the three-bedroomed house when there were just the two of them left. They might have hoped that he would one day return, but there was no way that Isaac could have come home.

His old room was depressing. There were still posters on the wall of Kelly McGillis in *Top Gun*, and of Kelly LeBrock in *Weird Science*. Joshua realised he must have had a thing back then for women called Kelly. It was a teenager's bedroom, and Joshua realised he had gone straight from being a teenager to a middle-aged man. He took off his shirt and trousers and flopped down on the single bed. It didn't take long for him to fall asleep.

It was dark when Joshua awoke. He looked at his mobile phone and saw that it was six o'clock – although he wasn't sure at first whether that was six in the morning or the evening. It turned out to be the evening. His head was pounding, and so he went through into the bathroom to pee and then to look in the medicine cabinet to see what painkillers his father had kept there before he died. Joshua realised that his day was getting better when he saw a packet of codeine and some diazepam, too. They would make a nice combination to get him through the rest of Christmas Day.

He swallowed two of each with water from the bathroom tap, and then went back into his bedroom and found his dressing gown. What was the point in getting dressed? He wasn't expecting any visitors.

Joshua walked through into the kitchen to make himself a cup of coffee, and then took it and sat down in front of the television in the living room. When he picked up the remote control from the coffee table, he saw that the box of stamps was there beside it. He stared at them, sure that he had dumped them into the wheelie bin outside. In fact, he knew he had put them there.

He leaned forward and poked at the box with his finger, not quite sure what he was expecting to happen. The lid didn't fly off, nothing jumped out at him, and the box didn't explode in his face – and yet he viewed it suspiciously. As he switched on the television, he though he heard a scratching sound coming from inside the box, but, when he muted the TV, the sound stopped, only to start again when he turned the volume back up. In fact, he thought that the scratching sound was getting louder.

Finally, he reached over and took the lid off the box, if only to satisfy his nerves. Inside were what must have been a dozen beetles, trying to claw their way up the inside of the box, and their legs making the scratching sound that he had been hearing. Joshua yelled, and stepped back from the box, not quite sure of what to do. Eventually, he plucked up the courage to put the lid back on the box, and then he went to the front door, opened it, and threw the box as far as he could into the garden. He knew it wouldn't come back this time.

Joshua shivered as he came back into the living room, not just from the cold, but because he was thoroughly creeped out by what had just happened. He turned the sound on the television back up, and tried to concentrate on the new Midsomer Murders episode that was the cornerstone of the channel's Christmas Evening schedule. The truth, however, was that he wasn't remotely interested. He didn't like the programme much anyway, and it had gone steadily downhill, he thought, since John Nettles had left it.

No, his mind was elsewhere, with the box of stamps and the beetles that were in it. They hadn't been there when he had opened the box the first time – but it was then that he had found one covered in blood. Joshua wondered if he was losing his mind. He went over to the window and looked out. He could see that the box of stamps was still in the middle of the overgrown lawn. And there, he hoped, it would stay.

In the end, Joshua gave up on the television and turned it off. He saw that he hadn't replaced the grille over the hole in the wall where he had found the stamp box, and he now felt a sudden urge to do so. He got down on the floor beside it, and couldn't stop himself from looking into the hole again before he started screwing the grille back on. He saw that there was something else in there, but he couldn't see what it was. Even the torch on his mobile phone didn't help a great

THE PHILATELIST

deal. It looked like a piece of paper, but it was right at the very back of the hole.

Joshua positioned himself on the floor so that he could put his entire arm into the gap. He wasn't happy doing so, fearing that there might be more spiders or beetles in there. He was never very good with insects, although he never let anyone know about his fear of them when he was younger. In fact, the only person who had known was Isaac, who, when he was small, asked Joshua to remove a spider from his room and he had refused.

Joshua slowly put his hand into the hole and started reaching for whatever was in there. More than once, he was tempted to give up, and then, finally, his hand touched the piece of paper. He grasped it and was about to pull his hand out when something took hold of it. It felt like another hand.

A cold, clammy, *dead* hand.

Joshua tried to pull away, but his arm was held firmly. He shrieked in fear, but it did him no good. And then there was a second hand, this time grabbing his wrist. And then a third gripping his elbow. They all felt the same, despite appearing to have emerged from different sides of the hole. He tried to tear his arm away from their grasp, but, as he did so, the hands that were grabbing him seemed to extend in length.

Finally, he freed his hand from the wall, falling onto his back as he did so. And, even then, he could still feel the touch of whatever had grabbed him. He got up off the floor as quickly as he could, and ran across to the far side of the room, half expecting to see a series of disembodied hands emerging from the dark hole. But none appeared. Perhaps he had imagined the entire thing. That must be it. He had a fever, and he was imagining things. And yet, when he looked down at his shirt sleeve, he saw a distinct print of a hand around his elbow, and a partial print on his wrist. Joshua Hale had not imagined it.

Joshua began to feel ill. A mix of the weirdness that was happening in the house, and too much whisky. As he ran through into the bathroom to throw up, he decided that there was no way that he was going to keep the house. He didn't believe in ghosts, or anything of that sort, but the shithole was going to be sold as quickly as possible. He didn't care if he got the highest price for it; he just wanted it off his hands.

He knelt down in front of the toilet, and vomited. He wiped his mouth, and then got up and went over to the sink, splashing cold water on to his face. He looked into the mirror, and realised he had rarely looked worse – and there had been times in his life when Joshua had been close to death. He tried to tell himself that everything he was experiencing was just in his imagination. Isaac was not coming back from the grave to get revenge on him after more than thirty years, on what would have been his fiftieth birthday. The date was what was playing on Joshua's mind. That had to be it. No other reason.

Joshua dried his face on the towel, and walked back into the living room. He nearly fainted at what he saw.

THE PHILATELIST

The box of stamps was back on the coffee table, but now the lid was lying beside it, and the walls were covered with hundreds – no, it must have been thousands, of stamps. Joshua wanted to just get out of the house and run, but he felt oddly compelled to walk over and look at them. There was no order to the stamps on the walls; it was more like a giant collage. Joshua put his hand on the wall, wondering if the stamps were still wet from having been glued to the wallpaper. But no, they were not. It was as if they had been there for years.

As he ran his hand over the stamps, he heard a noise from being him, coming from the hole in the wall. He turned around to watch as the noise got louder. And then he saw some grey, decomposing fingers emerge from it. And then the rest of a pair of hands. It simply wasn't possible. The hole in the wall was simply nowhere near big enough for that. The small box of stamps had barely fit in there. As Joshua watched, a pair of bare, grey arms appeared from the wall. And then, a head. Isaac's head. There was little flesh left on it, but it was unmistakably his.

Joshua stared in horror as the rest of his hideous, dead brother almost fell out of the hole in the wall on to the floor. Isaac was wearing the same clothes as on the day he died. His yellow T-shirt clung, damp and stained, to his ribcage, and the jeans hung low around his hips, almost falling off as he crawled – no, slithered – across the floor towards Joshua. As he did so, he smiled – the most revolting smile that Joshua had ever seen. He knew that he should just run out of the house and never come back, not even to sell it. What did money matter to him now? And yet, he was almost glued to the spot.

Finally, he managed to back away from the vile form that was coming towards him, but he only succeeded in reaching the window. He pushed himself as far up against it as he could, not screaming, but almost yelping in horror. A scream would not, *could not*, come from him at the moment. He was too terrified.

Anyone looking in from outside would simply have seen Joshua's back against the window, his arms flailing about, trying to push away something that no onlooker could see. But Joshua could see it. His brother was now kneeling on the floor, grabbing at Joshua's dressing gown, which fell open to reveal just the dirty boxer shorts that had been the only thing he had worn under it since his sleep earlier in the day.

Finally, the figure was standing in front of him, his face just inches away from Joshua's. He tried to scream, but again no sound came out. Isaac lifted his wet, decaying hand and pushed it on to Joshua's face. On to his mouth. The hand was full of stamps, and he forced them into Joshua's mouth. It wasn't just a handful, there must have been hundreds of stamps. Joshua couldn't tell where they were coming from, or how Isaac's ghost – for that is what it must have been – was managing to make them appear out of nowhere. But, as he choked as they were forced down his throat, Joshua saw that the stamps from the walls were disappearing. By the time he fell to the floor, there were none left. The last image he saw before losing consciousness was of the

THE PHILATELIST

decomposing body of his brother standing over him, and a final single stamp falling from his hand on to Joshua's face. And then came the sound of laughter.

★

When Joshua's body was found three days later, there was no sign of what had happened. The grille was back on the hole in the wall – and the box of stamps were back in there, too, and would be found by the new owners of the house. A post-mortem found that Joshua had choked on his own vomit after having consumed a large amount of alcohol. People in the village who remembered him as a teenager were not surprised. It was the type of ending they always thought he would have.

Only one strange thing was found during the post-mortem: a single stamp, lodged in Joshua Hale's windpipe. The pathologist, a stamp collector himself, was amazed to see it was a rare British £1 Postal Union Congress stamp from 1929, worth in the region of about £500. He said nothing about the stamp. Instead, he took it home, and added it to his own collection.

BREAKING UP IS HARD TO DO

The text message came at 11.43am. It was exactly the same time as it had appeared the previous year, and the year before that. Clara was, if nothing else, a creature of habit.

I had taken the phone out of my pocket that morning when I got to work, and placed it face down on the desk, so that the screen couldn't be seen – as if that would somehow prevent the inevitable from happening. I should have known better. After all, nothing had stopped the annual text before. I had tried everything. My mobile number had been changed often, and yet Clara had still managed to reach me. One year, I buried my phone in the garden, and the next morning on the bus it vibrated in my jacket pocket, where it most definitely had *not* been when I had left the house for work. It was covered with mud. In 2013, I had decided to go to London for the weekend to try and ignore December 21st. My theory had been that, if I wasn't in Norwich, then the yearly ritual *couldn't* take place. Walking along Tower Bridge early in the morning I had thrown my phone as far as I could into the Thames. An hour later, when I had gone back to my Travelodge room, it sat there on the pillow – soaked, smelling of the river, and yet still working. It seemed that nothing could stop the text coming, or the horrible events that would happen later in the day.

The phone vibrated its way along my desk. What would *really* happen if I just ignored it? I mean, *really* ignored it, no matter how many times the phone found its way back to me. Surely that would be the most sensible thing to do? It had been twenty-two years, for God's sake. Was this haunting – and there is no other word I can think of for it – really going to continue until the day I died?

I turned the phone over and looked down at the screen.

"Hello darling," it read. "I'm back in Norwich, now. Let's meet at The Turtle at 8.00. Love you lots. Clara. Xx"

The same as always.

The same as it had been twenty-two years earlier when Clara was very much alive, when these events were playing out for the first time.

The Turtle had been a public house in the centre of Norwich that was popular with students. But that had been a long time ago. It had gone through various name changes since then – hardly surprising given that The Turtle had always seemed like a stupid name for a pub. It had become The Black Cat, then the Goat's Head, and finally the somewhat more mundane Queen's Head. Now, it wasn't a pub at all, but a shop that sold those insufferable smelly candles and soaps. My sister had dragged me in there once when she had come to visit. I don't know how people can buy those things. All they do is make my nose run.

Despite all of that, at 8pm, when I went to meet Clara (*if* I went to meet Clara), it would once again be The Turtle pub. The bar staff and even the drink prices would be the same as they had been in 1998. I would recognise some of the people there – students I had been going to university with all those years ago. They would be the same age as they were then, and wearing the same clothes. The guys would be sporting the curtains haircut of the day, as if they were about to audition to form a new boyband. And Clara would be there, too. She would be sitting at the table closest to the roaring log fire. The conversation would continue, and then she would ask for a lift home. Everything would play out as before, and then I would wake up in bed at 7am on December 22nd, and it would all be over for another year. Just like it had been a dream.

But, looking down at the phone on my desk, I made the decision that this year would be different. I wasn't going to meet the young woman that had been killed when I crashed the car after drinking too much at The Turtle. That had been a terrible thing, a totally stupid thing, that I had regretted more than anyone could imagine. But I had paid for that. I'd been to prison. And, since my release, there had been this yearly ritual. It was time for me to end it.

Enough was enough.

I picked up the phone and replied to the text.

"Sorry, I'm not able to make it."

No kisses.

At last. I had made the first move to finishing this thing. It made me feel better. I got up from my chair, walked out of my office and went to the gents. I threw the phone at the tiled wall, and then picked it up from the floor and did it again. It was still working, and so it then got smashed down repeatedly onto the rim of one of the sinks. When it fell on the floor in several pieces, I went over and stamped on it repeatedly. If felt so good. I leaned against the wall and took a deep breath just as one of the cubicle doors opened. I smiled meekly at Marcus who worked in the office next door to me. I hadn't even bothered to check if I was alone in there.

"You're hoping for a new phone for Christmas, then?" he joked as he washed his hands.

"Something like that."

He walked out of the door, no doubt bemused by my actions. I gathered together the various pieces of the phone and dropped some into each of the three toilets and then flushed. This was it. This year the appalling ritual would come to an end.

I took a couple of minutes to calm down, and then went back to my office. The phone was back on my desk

– soaking wet, but whole once again. A text message read:

"Don't be silly. Of course, you'll come. See you tonight. Xx."

Shaking, I sat down and wiped the mobile phone dry with a tissue.

The fog had begun to descend again. It was always foggy when I went to meet Clara, but normally just for an hour or so as I walked to the pub that was no longer there. This year, the fog was real. It had descended on the streets of Norwich a few days earlier, and had stubbornly stayed there ever since. It would lift for maybe a couple of hours each day, as the weak winter sun attempted to burn through it. It was a valiant effort, but the fog always returned shortly after it had lifted.

My hatred of the fog had started when I was a kid. It had always given me the creeps back then, but I never knew why. Perhaps it had been something on television that had scared me, but there was always that feeling that there could be something unseen and unpleasant about to grab me at any moment. That feeling had not gone away as I got older – especially since it had been foggy on the night of the accident, and for every date with Clara on December 21st since.

I decided not to take a lunch hour, at least that way I could go home early instead. Our manager didn't mind if we did that. Not much work would get done anyway with just a few days to Christmas. I spent the afternoon thinking about what was going to happen that evening. Would I go to The Turtle and see Clara, or have the guts to stay at home instead, not knowing what would happen if I did? I had never taken that option before – even when I was in London for the weekend, the year my phone ended up in the Thames, I had bottled it and hurried home on the train so that I could get to the pub in time. Eventually, the decision was made. I would go to The Turtle, meet Clara and tell her that this had to stop. Could you reason with a ghost? Perhaps ask for forgiveness? It seemed that that evening would be the time to try.

On getting home from work, I forced myself to eat a sandwich and have a cup of tea – everything seemed better after a cup of tea – and then I lied down for half an hour or so, preparing myself for what was to come. After changing my clothes, I left home at 7.30. My aim was to scurry along the foggy streets of Norwich and get to the pub as quickly as possible. As always, the fog played tricks on me. The strange acoustics of the weather meant that it was impossible to tell if the footsteps that were heard echoing around me were my own or if they were from someone following me. More than a few times, I had turned around and peered into the greyness behind me, hoping that there would be no-one or nothing there waiting for me.

There was a certain irony to my fear of the fog, for in my spare time, I wrote ghost stories. My name was not known by the public at large, but many had heard my work as I was a regular contributor to *Mystery at Midnight*, a radio series of fifteen-minute mystery and supernatural tales that had been running every weeknight for forty years. Audience numbers were much smaller than they used to be – who listened to Radio Four these days? – but when the B.B.C. had made public its plan to axe the series, there was an outcry, led by a popular tabloid that ran a "Mercy for Mystery at Midnight" campaign – tabloids love alliteration. The B.B.C's decision was overturned, which helped me somewhat, for each of my stories that were broadcast resulted in a very welcome, if undeniably modest, payment into my bank account. I didn't narrate the stories himself, leaving that to others, including some rather impressive showbiz names over the years: Judi Dench, Stephen Fry, Hannah Gordon, Angela Rippon – and Harry from McFly. In truth, I had no real idea who this Harry was, but my niece was very excited at the time, even if she ended up being repulsed by the story. Little did she know that her Uncle Leonard had got the inspiration for his ghost stories from real life. During the campaign to save the series, I had once been referred to by a journalist as the "M. R. James of our generation," which pleased me somewhat, even if I knew deep down that I was nothing of the sort. And, even if the title had been true, it didn't help much. It was the office job that paid the bills, not my literary efforts.

 With trepidation, I turned into the small street that housed the candle and soap shop that had once been The Turtle pub. While I was hoping to see the shop that was *really* there, I also realised there was little chance of that. It had never happened in previous years. Peering through the fog as I approached, the lights coming from inside the pub soon became visible. I stood still for a moment, readying myself for what was to follow. My aim was to go inside, find Clara, tell her it was over, and then leave as soon as possible. It was time for this to stop.

It was hot and sweaty inside the pub, just as it had been the first time the events had occurred – and every year since. There were more people there than was normal for The Turtle, but that was only to be expected just a few days before Christmas. Looking around, I recognised several faces. They were people who, like me, had thought the best thing to do during the Christmas vacation of their final year of university was to stay in Norwich rather than travel home. Essays had to be written, dissertations had to be started, and revision for the January exams was on lots of people's minds. A couple of fellow students waved at me, or nodded in acknowledgement. I waved or nodded back, forcing a smile, although doing so seemed ridiculous as they were not really there. Like me, in real life they were not twenty-one any longer – but that wasn't the case in the pub. As could easily be seen on Facebook, most of the people there now had receding hairlines, or were about three or four stone heavier. In some cases, both. Did I also look young to the people around me that evening? Presumably so, or their ghosts – if you could have a ghost of a living person – wouldn't have recognised me. For a moment, I thought about going into the gents to look at myself to find out. But no, that would have been a distraction. Tonight wasn't about satisfying my curiosity regarding the ghost world I found myself in for one evening every year, it was about never having to go there again.

"You want the usual, Len?" the barman asked me.

"Not tonight, thanks," I replied. "I'm not stopping."

Clara was in her usual place by the fire. The most uncomfortable table in the pub during the winter, and yet she had always sat there when we had gone to The Turtle for a drink. I hated that spot, for my face would always feel like it was burning after a short while there. Clara was wearing the same clothes that she had the first time. Her hair style was the same, too. Nothing had changed. Nothing ever did.

"I thought you were never coming over," Clara said to me, when I went over to her. "I thought you were just going to stay at the bar all night."

Like everyone else in The Turtle, Clara didn't look like a ghost. She wasn't see-through, nor was she surrounded in a strange spirit glow or aura. She looked as alive as everyone else. If I had by chance wandered into that pub on that night, I never would have known. But, of course, that was partly the point. Nobody could have gone in there by chance that night – because it didn't exist.

It was time for me to act.

"You can stop the pretense, Clara," I stammered. "I'm not staying here tonight. I'm not going to do this ever again. This is over."

Clara looked hurt.

"You're breaking up with me? Three days before

Christmas?" she said. "What has got into you? Have I done something wrong?"

"You're *dead.*"

"Are you threatening me?" Clara asked, standing up. "Why would you say a thing like that?"

"I'm not threatening you. I'm telling you. Don't you even *know*?"

"Know what? What are you talking about?"

"Clara, you are *dead.*"

I said the words just as whatever song was playing ended, and they came out louder than I had planned. Half the pub heard me, and the crowd went quiet. Clara sat down again, trying to hide the smile that was on her lips. Nobody else could see it, but I knew it was there. She was enjoying herself.

Jack, a fellow student back in the day, walked over to me.

"Everything alright?" he asked.

"Everything's fine," I said, trying not to look at the younger version of my former friend who was now married to a journalist for the Daily Mail. It wasn't just my life that had gone to shit.

"Perhaps you should go home," Jack said, trying to be Clara's knight in shining armour. "Perhaps you've had a bit too much to drink, eh?"

I thought for a moment and then nodded. Yes. It *was* time for me to go home and put this behind me for good.

Perhaps breaking up with Clara was what I should have done before. If I broke up with her, she wouldn't get in my car, and then she wouldn't die. *Was that right?* That I could possibly change history? Instead of haunting me, had Clara really been giving me the chance each year to do things differently? Surely it couldn't be that easy?

"Yes," I said. "I'll go home. Had a bit too much in the uni bar. Goodbye, Clara."

I put my hand on Jack's shoulder, forced a smile at Clara and then turned around and started walking towards the door. At that point, whatever song was playing through the speakers abruptly stopped, and in its place came an old rock 'n' roll love song: Neil Sedaka's *Breaking Up is Hard to Do*. It had been a sing-a-long classic for sixty years, but right then those lyrics seemed like a threat. There was no doubt in my mind that Clara had caused the track to play at that precise moment, and much louder than the previous songs, to make sure I heard it. I turned around once more to look at her. She was laughing with Jack – perhaps laughing about me. She saw me turn and winked. She knew that her message had been received – walking away and moving on was going to be far harder than I had first thought. She would make sure of that.

I went outside, pulling the door shut behind me. Walking away, I knew instinctively that the pub was no longer there, and was back to being the shop that it was now. Was that a good thing or bad? It certainly meant there was no turning back – no way of going back in and making up with Clara. My decision had been made and now I had to live with it.

Oddly, I didn't feel particularly frightened by what had happened. I had, after all, gone through meeting Clara every year since I had been released from prison. Even walking through the fog on my way home didn't unnerve me. When I got home, I went straight into the lounge and poured myself a stiff drink. And then another. I went for a shower, as if I thought that it would somehow cleanse me after having been with the ghosts of the past for a few minutes. That was all it had been: a few minutes. Normally the horrible events of December 21st lasted much longer than that. I would let Clara lead the conversation, and just let myself replay the events of before. It felt good to have changed that pattern, to have made my own move for once, although whether it would do me any good or not remained to be seen.

After showering, I got dry and then pulled on a dressing gown and went downstairs to make a cup of tea. I went into the kitchen, and found that my phone was on the bench beside the kettle. I didn't remember putting it there – in fact I was sure it should still have been in my coat pocket. My stomach churned when I saw that there was a text message.

"Are you sure you really want to end this?" it read.

I texted back.

"Yes. Sorry."

With that, the smart speaker that sat on top of the fridge lit up and started playing the same song that I had heard in the pub as I was leaving.

And breaking up is hard to do...

BREAKING UP IS HARD TO DO

I shouted, "Alexa, stop!"

It kept playing. I tried again.

"Alexa, stop!"

"I'm sorry, I don't know how to do that."

It was Clara's voice coming through the speaker.

The song didn't stop playing, and I knew from the experience with my phone that breaking or smashing the speaker would not help, and so I picked it up, went out of the back door, and placed it in the shed at the bottom of the garden. I knew it couldn't get loud enough to be heard in the house, but I was naïve to think that something so simple would end everything. When I went back in the house, the same song was playing through the TV speakers. I quickly turned it off and unplugged it.

This was the point when I began to believe that I had made a mistake. I might have walked out on Clara in the pub, but now she had followed me home, and this had not happened before.

Having poured myself a third drink, I sat down in the armchair. I closed my eyes, hoping that I would doze off to sleep, and then awaken the next day when everything would be over. After a few minutes, I felt myself drifting off, but at that point, the TV switched back on. I was awake instantly. The local news was playing, but the newsreader on the television had not appeared on our screens for at least the previous fifteen years. In the top right corner of the screen was a picture of Clara. She was smiling, and looking beautiful. I remembered that photo being taken at a party we had gone to about a year before she died. It had been a wonderful night. Clara always loved a party, and, in many ways, parties loved Clara. She knew how to let her hair down without getting rowdy or overly drunk. She was the perfect guest.

The newsreader said:

"The police are appealing for witnesses after the A47 just outside Thorpe St Andrew was closed for several hours last night following an accident which left one person dead and another in hospital. The dead woman has been named as 20-year-old Clara Gaskill, a student at the University of East Anglia."

I swear that, as the story ended, the photo of Clara changed. She moved so that she was staring right at me. And then the expression changed, too, so that she was giving that strange, knowing smile that I had seen just before I left the pub.

The television turned itself off, and the house became totally quiet. I sat still, not daring to move. Nothing happened, not a sound could be heard. For a moment, I thought that, if I moved, it would somehow trigger something else to happen.

I got up from the chair and went over to the window. Pulling the curtains apart slightly, I looked outside. The fog seemed to be denser than ever. It wasn't even possible to see the streetlamp that was only ten metres or so away. I began to feel claustrophobic, even trapped. I had the fear that Clara would appear in person at any moment, and that I would have nowhere to run – if, indeed, running was likely to do me any good. There was, it seemed to me at the time, an inevitability about what was happening. I closed the curtains again, making sure that there were no gaps through which I would be able to see something moving outside.

Sitting back down again, I realised that I had one thing left to try. I couldn't go back to The Turtle to try to reverse my decision to walk out on Clara, but perhaps I could contact her in the same way she contacted me. I took my mobile phone out of my trouser pocket and replied to Clara's last text. My hands trembled as I typed:

"I'm sorry, Clara, I don't know what I was thinking. Are you still at The Turtle? I could come back?"

I put the phone down on the table and started pacing up and down the room.

Had I done the right thing?

Those moments after I had sent the text seemed to last forever. My feeling of being trapped continued to grow, and my mind seemed to start working overtime. What if she didn't reply? What if she *did*? Would I have to go out into the fog and meet her again at The Turtle? Would the night still be able to play out as it always did? That was something I had desperately been trying to avoid earlier in the day, and yet now it seemed like something that would be the best possible outcome. At least I knew how that ended.

The phone vibrated and I picked it up and read the message on the screen.

"Yes, I'm still here. I thought you might change

your mind. Bring the car, and you can drive me home."

I knew that I couldn't do that, not after the amount I had drunk since I had got home. There wouldn't be an accident taking Clara back home this time – instead, it would be before I even got to the pub.

"I can't drive you home," I texted back. "I've been drinking."

"It never stopped you before."

"Perhaps it should have done," I wrote.

I waited to see what Clara's next move might be.

"Don't worry," the next text read. "I'll come to the house instead."

I put the phone back in my pocket. Now I had to wait for her to arrive. If I had lived on a main road, I would have run out of the house and flagged down a taxi, telling them to just keep driving until morning. I didn't want Clara in my house. If she came there, I wondered if she would ever leave. My house had never been remotely involved in the haunting up until now. Would I even want to live there afterwards? I would be afraid that Clara was going to appear at any moment.

These were all questions I would have to answer later. My main aim was merely to get through the night. This was unchartered territory. My mind was racing. At one moment I felt certain that I would not be alive to see tomorrow, that Clara would make sure of that. And a moment later, I was convincing myself that everything would be just fine in the end. After all, if Clara wanted me dead, she'd had plenty of opportunities to make that happen – and yet, no matter how frightening and disturbing the annual event could be, I had never come to physical harm. These questions kept going around and around in my head.

I kept as quiet as I could, in the hope that I would hear something to give me a warning that Clara was here. But there was nothing. Despite not living in a busy area, most nights you would at least here a car drive past, or perhaps one of the other people on the street coming home from their night out. Tonight, there wasn't a sound. Perhaps everyone had stayed in because of the fog, but it was only a few days to Christmas and so that seemed unlikely. I felt as if I was almost holding my breath, waiting for something to happen – just like one of the characters in my own ghost stories.

Finally, I heard footsteps coming towards the house. They sounded louder than normal – the fog was playing its acoustic tricks again. I prepared myself for them to come up the footpath to my house, but they didn't. They went straight past and continued further up the road. A false alarm. I breathed a sigh of relief.

At that moment the radio burst to life. An announcer said:

"A reminder that tonight's *Mystery at Midnight* will be *Breaking Up Is Hard to Do*, written by Leonard Elder and read by the author. That is at midnight tonight, here on Radio Four."

But I had never written a story with that title, and I'd never read my own stories on air either. The guest narrators were part of the appeal of the series.

GHOST STORIES FOR CHRISTMAS

The radio started to skip between stations. Bits of songs would play here and there, and then there would be a few seconds of commentary on a football match, and then something from a news broadcast. Finally, it went silent. I breathed a sigh of relief, only for the radio to then come back on, this time at full volume, playing, again, *Breaking Up Is Hard to Do*. I went over to it quickly and turned it off, and was surprised when the radio actually went quiet.

I didn't know what to do. I was beginning to feel oddly disoriented...and hot. I felt sweat start trickling down my face, and I could feel that the back of my shirt was wet through sweat as well. I assumed that it was a panic attack. Having one at that moment would hardly be unexpected, and while I didn't suffer from them frequently, I did have them from time to time. Perhaps the three drinks I'd had weren't helping things, either. I tried to do some breathing exercises. I needed to open a window or a door and get some fresh air in – I knew from the past that that might help – but that was the last thing I wanted to do at that point, knowing that Clara was on her way.

I went into the kitchen and ran the cold tap, splashing the water over my face to try and cool me down, but it didn't help. The room had started to spin, and I was beginning to get unsteady on my feel. I felt that I needed to sit down, or maybe even call for an ambulance. I stumbled into the hallway and was about to go back into the living room when there were three loud knocks at the front door. I froze. There was no doubt in my mind who – or what – it was, but I just wanted to get things over with. I fell towards the front door, and unlocked it, while the room still spun around me. As I pulled the door open, I felt the most tremendous pain in my chest. My knees buckled and I fell to the floor. And then…darkness.

★

I opened my eyes to see a nurse looking down at me.

"Mr. Elder?" she asked.

I nodded.

"That's good. How are you feeling?"

I ran my tongue over my lips.

"Water," I muttered.

"Just a little," the nurse said.

She picked up a glass of water from the table beside my bed and I took a few sips.

"Not too much."

I nodded.

"What happened?"

"You had a heart attack. You were brought in at about ten o'clock last night. You were awake, but you may not remember anything."

I shook my head. I remembered nothing after the pain in my chest when I was opening the front door. I had never for a minute thought that I might be having a heart attack.

"You may remember later," the nurse said. "But you're going to be fine. You were lucky that someone saw it happen and called the ambulance for you."

"Clara?" I asked.

The nurse must have wondered why I looked so scared when I spoke the name.

"Is that your wife? Girlfriend?"

I shook my head.

"No," the nurse said. "It was a pizza delivery man. He knocked on your door, as he saw the light was on and he couldn't find the address he was looking for due to the fog. He thought you might be able to help. I wonder if the fog will ever lift. But at least you can't see it in here."

I couldn't believe it. I was alive. I had got through the night after all.

At that moment, a man walked into the room, with a few others following him.

"Ah," said the nurse. "That's Dr. Renault on his rounds. He'll be over here in a few minutes. He's got some students with him, but don't worry about them. It's just part of their training."

I smiled.

"Thank you," I said.

The nurse walked away, and I closed my eyes. I must have drifted back to sleep, for when I opened them again, the doctor was pulling the curtain around the bed.

"Mr. Elder, isn't it? You had a heart attack last night. Nothing too severe, I'm pleased to say. These are student doctors; I hope that's all right with you."

"Of course. I don't mind them being here with you."

BREAKING UP IS HARD TO DO

It was true. I remember thinking at that point that as long as I was going to get better, I didn't care who was gathered around my bed when the doctor did his rounds. But I regretted thinking that a few seconds later, when another person slipped in behind the student doctors and closed the curtains behind her. She turned around and smiled at me. There *was* one person I didn't want at my bedside, and she was staring right at me.

THE STRANGER IN THE SNOW

The cottage was perfect. It was exactly what I was looking for – somewhere that I could rent for a few months in order to write up the research that I had been working on for well over a year. The research itself had gone well, but I was struggling to get my findings down on paper.

My wife and I had no children of our own, but my brother and sister-in-law had been killed in a car accident about two years earlier, and their two children had been living with us ever since. If truth be told, that was the main reason why the monograph was so difficult to write.

I was used to a quiet house, but now, with a ten-year-old and eight-year-old running around, it was anything but. Of course, the house would normally have been quiet during the day, and I could have worked then, but that wasn't the case during the pandemic, when kids were staying at home rather than going to school – and people like me were being encouraged to work from home, also.

It was Susan, my wife, who had come up with the idea of me finding a cheap, quiet house somewhere, so that I could get my work done. She suggested that I go and stay there during the week and come home at the weekends. A couple of years earlier, we wouldn't have been able to afford it, but my brother and his wife had left us a considerable amount of money, and so my "moving out" seemed less of an extravagance than it would have done before, and Susan was rather enjoying parenting in a way that I most definitely was not – even if I had nothing against the two children who were now in our care.

Susan and I had always wanted children of our own, but it had never happened – although it wasn't through a lack of trying. Various options had been open to us – IVF, and so on – but we had chosen not to go down those routes. We were very much of the view that, if it happened, then great. Otherwise, we wouldn't be bitterly unhappy. Perhaps fate had stepped in, and we hadn't had children of our own for the reason that we would become the guardians of my brother's children at a later date. I'm no great believer in fate, but sometimes you do have to wonder, considering how things work out.

After being shown around the cottage, I told the letting agent that I would like it for three months –

which was the least amount of time that the owner would consider renting it for. It was a nice property – too large, really, with three bedrooms – but it was only about ten miles away from my wife and the children. Despite this, the cottage was, in many respects, in the middle of nowhere. It was two miles from the nearest village, and had no bus route running close by. The letting agent told me that it had been part of a school at one point, but the other buildings (including the main school building) had burned down back in the 1970s. It didn't seem strange to me at the time that nothing had been built on the land in the intervening years. Apparently, that land now came with the cottage that I was to rent, and that suited me just fine. It meant that there would be no disturbances from neighbours.

When I got home after the viewing and told my wife the news, she seemed overjoyed, although she questioned whether there was really much point in going with just ten days or so to Christmas, but I said I wanted to get started straight away. Perhaps other men might have felt put out that their wife was happy that they were moving out for a few months, but our work was important to both of us. We told the children over supper than night that I would be going to live in the cottage during the week and returning at weekends, and the arrangement would begin on the following Monday. The kids thought, at first, that this was our way of saying we were getting divorced, but we reiterated that was not the case.

The weather forecasters had been saying all

weekend that there would be heavy snow-storms on the Monday afternoon, and so I set off reasonably early to avoid them. I arrived at the cottage at about ten o'clock in the morning, and, by midday, I had unpacked what few things I had brought, and had got settled in somewhat. There was an old writing desk in one of the bedrooms, and so I set my laptop up on that, and managed to turn the rest of the room into a usable office. I filled the fridge in the kitchen with the food and milk I had brought with me, and plugged a blu-ray player into the television in the living room. I might have finished the research element of my project but there would still be a need to re-watch films (or parts of films) that I was writing about. The box of DVDs and blu-rays that I had brought with me were unpacked and placed on some empty shelves that were in the living room.

Given that it was approaching midday, I decided that I would have an early lunch and then start work in the afternoon. I realized that there was no microwave in the kitchen, and debated whether it would be a good idea to buy a cheap one from Amazon, given that cooking was hardly something I was good at. Still, I had no objection to living on beans on toast if I had to. About twenty minutes later, I was sitting in front of the television, watching the news while I ate. There was much doom and gloom, not just about the virus, but also about the forthcoming bad weather, which was supposedly about two hours away from where I was. I was, oddly, rather looking forward to it. The remoteness of the cottage made me feel that any such snow storm could be quite impressive to watch. Perhaps it would put me in the right frame of mind to write about the old horror films I had been researching.

I got up from the chair, went into the kitchen to wash up, and then went upstairs and switched on my laptop, opening the box file of notes while it booted up. I took out the large stacks of papers and placed them on the table next to the computer. A picture of Conrad Veidt in *The Man who Laughs* stared up at me. It was a print-out of the front page of a movie magazine from the late 1920s. The film had always given me the creeps, despite the fact that it was not a horror film in the strictest sense. It was really a historical melodrama based on a Victor Hugo novel, with Veidt playing a man who had been disfigured after a wide grin was carved on to his face as a boy. I found it far more disturbing than any film featuring Dracula, Frankenstein's monster or the Wolf Man. I turned the page over so that I didn't have to look at it.

While the laptop chugged away as it booted up, I went over to the CD player I had brought with me, and inserted a disc and started it playing. I bought too much music – I was well aware of that – and much of it I never got around to listen to. Now was the perfect opportunity to catch up. I had brought with me a large, boxed set issued by Decca of some fifty or so discs of opera and lieder recitals, some of which went back to the 1940s. I hadn't had the chance to play them at home, and so was looking forward to ploughing through them during the coming weeks. I made up my mind to start with the first disc and work through them in order.

With the disc playing, I opened the Word document that contained what little work I had completed on my book. I read through it a couple of times, and decided that I would delete the whole thing and start again. It wasn't that the few thousand words I had written were particularly bad, but they weren't particularly good, either. I felt that I needed a fresh start. With a new file opened, I started typing.

After an hour or so, I had written about eight-hundred words, and was pleased that I had got into something of a rhythm. I didn't really want to stop while the going was good, but the bathroom was calling, and so I saved my work, went to the bathroom and then made my way downstairs to make a cup of tea. As I went back upstairs to the room in which I was working, I realized that it was getting darker outside, and it was clear that the bad weather that had been forecast was fast approaching. The view from the window in front of me was rather impressive. The snow clouds were making their way across the fens towards the cottage. The wind had certainly got up, and the couple of trees in the garden of the cottage were being battered by what had now become a gale.

I was almost mesmerised seeing the clouds approach in this way, and the progress I had made with my work just an hour before was now halted by the spectacle outside. The snow was beginning to fall now, and it splattered against the window with considerable force due to the heavy wind. I closed the screen of my laptop, knowing that I wouldn't be able to concentrate until the snow had passed – or, at least, until it was dark outside, or I had got bored by it. I just sat there, watching the storm play out.

It didn't take long for the ground to be covered in snow, and, after a relatively short amount of time, I realized that I could easily be snowed in if it continued to fall for many hours. Perhaps that was what I needed in order to get my work done. As the CD I was playing came to a halt, I thought that perhaps I should ring Susan and make sure she was alright.

"What's it like where you are?" she asked me after we had said hello.

"The snow's falling at quite a rate," I told her. "But it's very beautiful out here in the middle of nowhere. No, not beautiful exactly. But…"

"Picturesque?" Susan asked.

"Something like that, I suppose. I'm a bit worried I might get snowed in."

"At least you'll have no excuse to not get your work done."

"Well, unless there's a power cut," I said.

"Yes, that's true," Susan said, a little concerned. "Just keep everything charged up as much as you can. Your phone and your laptop."

"I've already thought of that. How are the kids?" I asked.

"They're outside building a snowman in the back garden. I'm quite glad the schools have already finished for Christmas. It stops any of that will-they-or-won't-they be open or closed rubbish. But all is fine here."

A minute or two later, I ended the call, buoyed by my brief contact with the outside world, even if I had only been away from it for six hours or so. I plugged the mobile phone back into its charger – at least I'd have a day of two's worth of battery if the electric went off.

By now, it was nearly dark, and I went through the house, drawing the curtains, doing my best to keep the heat in and the cold out. As I did so in the living room, I thought I saw someone – or something – pass through the garden. I would have said *walk* through the garden, but whatever it was didn't seem to be grounded. I wondered if it was a large bird of some kind, perhaps even an owl. I peered out through the window, but it was too dark to see anything properly, and so I tried to forget about what I had seen.

I went through into the kitchen and thought that, now I had stopped work for a while, I should think about what to have for supper. I soon learned in the coming days at the cottage, that, when living alone and having stopped working, the mind generally thinks about food. In the fridge was a shepherd's pie, which Susan had made the week before, and frozen. I thought it would be particularly suitable for such a cold, snowy evening, and so I switched on the oven and went back into the living room while it reached its desired temperature.

I switched on the television, and sat through the daily statistics about the virus that was on the news channels, and then watched the reports about the weather conditions. It was going to get worse before it got better, the weatherman told us, and I realized that I should get prepared to be stuck in the cottage for several days unless the rest of the storm somehow bypassed us. I sneaked another peak out of the window, and saw that the snow was still falling, and it wouldn't be long before the country roads would be impassable. It seemed to take less snow each winter for this to happen.

A couple of hours passed as I ate the shepherd's pie in front of the television while watching a rather dismal 1940s B-movie that was being shown on one of the cable channels. I had seen worse – much worse – as part of my research, but, even so, this was very much a watch-because-there's-nothing-better-on type of film.

When the film ended, I washed up the plate that I had just used, and was about to go back upstairs to start work again when there was a knock on the front door. Surprised that anyone would be out in the inclement weather, I went to the door and opened it.

Standing in front of me was a policeman. A constable, I thought. He certainly didn't seem to act with an air of authority, and almost seemed embarrassed to be there.

"Good evening," I said. "Can I help you?"

"I'm sorry to trouble you, Sir," the constable said. "But I was wondering if I might take a moment or two of your time?"

"Of course. Please come in."

The constable smiled at me and then came into the hallway, wiping his feet thoroughly on the doormat.

"It's not getting any better outside, then?" I asked,

trying to break the ice a little.

"Not at all, Sir," the policeman said. "It's very nasty outside."

"Come through into the living room," I said. "You'll find it much warmer in there."

He followed me through into the living room and I told him to sit down, which he did.

"Would you like something to drink? A tea or coffee, perhaps? Something to warm you up?"

"No, Sir," the constable replied. "I cannot stop long. I want to get back to the village. Before it gets too late."

"Too late for what?"

"I meant the weather, Sir. The roads will be blocked in a couple of hours at most, and I don't fancy walking home."

"Of course." I sat down in the chair opposite him. "So, how can I help you?" I asked.

"Well, that depends. How long are you planning to be staying in the cottage, Sir?"

"Two or three months, I think. I have work to type up, and I'm not getting on very well at home, and so I have rented the cottage to give me some peace and quiet."

"Ah! I see!" the policeman said. "And you're not from around this area to start with?"

"No, not really. We live in the city. So about ten miles away."

"I see," he said, again. "Well, I figured as much, and so I thought it would be a good time to come and have a little chat with you."

THE STRANGER IN THE SNOW

"About what? Have I done anything wrong?"

"Oh no. Nothing wrong, Sir. But with the weather as it is, I was wondering if you might be able to help us. We are keeping an eye out for a young man, you see? And I was thinking that you might see him?"

"I only arrived this morning," I said. "And I haven't seen anyone. Hardly surprising given the weather. But I don't think anyone lives close by, do they?"

"No, indeed."

"So, has this young man gone missing?" I asked.

The policeman seemed to tense up when I asked this question.

"Not yet, Sir," he said, quietly.

I was rather surprised by his odd reply.

"Not yet?" I queried.

"Indeed, Sir."

"But you're expecting it to happen? I'm afraid that I don't understand."

I wondered if I was being a bit slow on the uptake, but I believed that I was not. Why would a policeman come to my door in order to tell me about someone that might go missing but hadn't yet? The conversation was not making sense.

The policeman took a moment to try and gather his thoughts.

"We have reason to think that a teenaged boy of maybe seventeen or eighteen will go missing at some point in the following day or two, and that he will likely come here."

I stared at him, and wondered if he was actually a

policeman at all. Perhaps I had inadvertently let a mad man into the cottage.

"Here?" I asked.

"I realise this sounds very strange, Sir," the policeman went on. "But the truth of the matter is that this has happened before in this kind of weather, and with the road to the village likely to be blocked by morning, we thought it was worth coming to see you in advance."

"You're telling me that when it snows, teenage boys go missing from the village?"

The policeman nodded his head.

"That's correct, Sir."

"And they come here?"

"Yes."

"Will this boy be dangerous?"

"Oh no, Sir, not at all."

"How do you know? He might have a concealed weapon."

"That's unlikely."

"Why?"

"Because, in previous years, there have been no weapons involved."

"Can I ask why this is going to happen?"

"I'd rather you didn't," the policeman said, rising to his feet. "It would probably be for the best if I went now, or the car won't get back along the roads."

He walked back into the hallway, and I opened the front door for him.

"Look after yourself, Sir," he said. "And if the boy

does turn up, it would be appreciated if you'd look after him. Keep him warm, and all that. Good night, Sir."

And, with that, he was gone.

I shut the door and went back into the living room, rather bemused by the conversation. If I was being totally honest, I would say that the policeman seemed thoroughly embarrassed by the information he had relayed to me, and yet had seemed perfectly earnest.

I telephoned Susan and told her about the episode.

"Do you think someone's playing a trick on me?" I asked her.

"Not on you," Susan said. "But on him. I bet someone in the station had made a bet with him or dared him to come and tell you that story. Something like that. I'm sure that's all it was."

"Well, it was very bad timing," I said. "He could have had an accident getting here in the snow."

"You know what some people are like. They don't think about things like that. It was just a lark. I bet that you'll find out for sure before you come home for Christmas."

I wasn't quite so certain, but we said goodnight to each other, and ended the call. It was around ten o'clock by this point and, although I was normally someone who didn't go to bed until the early hours, I felt decidedly sleepy, and decided to turn in. It had been a busy – not to mention, slightly odd – day, and I thought I would feel better the next day if I had a good night's sleep.

Sadly, sleep didn't come quickly, and I found myself

lying awake going over what the policeman had said while he was at the cottage. The more I went over it, the more I decided that it was not just some strange prank. He had been genuinely worried that a young lad might try to come to the cottage in the snow.

I got out of bed and went through into the room that I had made into my office. I switched on the computer and, rather miraculously, found that the internet was still working. I tried doing a Google search for missing teenagers from the village during previous winters, but I found none, although I realized that we hadn't really had bad snow since the so-called "beast from the east" a few years back. And so, I centred my search around that period in early 2018, in order to see if that brought up any results. There wasn't much, but there was a couple of small articles in the local newspaper. The first one reported that a young man was missing from the village, and the second one, from a couple of days later, informed readers that he had been found a couple of miles away, and that he was suffering from hypothermia, but was expected to make a full recovery.

I set about finding out which years had had heavy snowfall in the local area, and then seeing if I could find similar articles from the local newspapers about missing boys. There certainly seemed to be some correlation, going back several decades. There wasn't always an article with every snowfall, but I assumed that the newspapers weren't informed if the person had been found quickly.

THE STRANGER IN THE SNOW

The whole thing seemed very strange indeed, but I realised that I wouldn't find out much more simply through using the internet. I needed to speak to someone local who could give me more information.

I had begun to get sleepy, and so went back to bed, but not before looking out of each window to make sure I couldn't see a boy outside.

*

I woke up at about nine o'clock the next morning, and was quite surprised that I had managed to sleep right through the night, especially given it was my first night in the cottage and with the strange events of the previous evening.

The cottage didn't have a shower, and so I ran a bath while I shaved and cleaned my teeth. The hot water system was barely adequate, and so the bath needed a couple of kettles of boiling water to make it hot enough. But once it was full, I soaked in it for at least half an hour, basking in the silence that was now only rarely present in my own house. I loved my brother's kids, but I loved the peace and quiet we had before they moved in with us, too. I thought of this while I was laying there in the tub, and I felt saddened by my own selfish thoughts. Those kids had lost their parents, and I was moaning to myself about the house being noisier.

Eventually, I got out of the bath, got dressed, and went downstairs to fix some breakfast, opening the curtains in the downstairs rooms while I prepared the food. The snow had been falling heavily all night, and it was still coming down. When looking out of the kitchen window, there was no way of knowing where the garden path ended and the grass began. The same was true out of the front window. The garden, the footpath, the road and the field on the other side were all merged into one. And standing about five or ten metres from the window, was a boy.

I had forgotten – or, at least, tried to forget – the weird visit from the policeman the night before. A night of sleep had rather put it to the back of my mind. I peered out of the window to make sure that he was really there, and not some strange optical illusion caused by the snow. But he was definitely there, and staring directly at me. He wasn't moving, just standing still – not affected in any way by the cold weather, it seemed. He wore no coat, and was there in his shirtsleeves and trousers. I guessed that he was about eighteen years old, but it was difficult to be sure.

I went into the hallway, put on some boots and a coat, and opened the front door. It was like a blizzard. It wasn't just the snow, but the wind, which was blowing directly towards the house. I was covered in snow in an instant. But I had to go and get the boy indoors.

I went outside and pulled the door shut behind me. As I trudged towards him, I saw that the boy wasn't moving at all – not even shivering. I thought for a moment that he might be dead already from the cold, but then I saw the breath coming from his mouth. I grabbed hold of his hand, trying to lead him into the cottage. He refused to move, as if he was in some kind of trance, and so I picked him up and carried him inside, closing the front door behind me.

By now, I could see that he was indeed about eighteen years old, slightly built, and, while he was wearing shirt and trousers, he had on neither socks nor shoes. I put him down on the sofa in front of the fire while I worked out what I should do with him.

My first thought was to call the police or an ambulance, but there was no mobile reception, probably due to the weather, and the house had no landline phone. I ran upstairs and turned the computer on, but guessed that the internet would probably be down, too. I wondered if I could get him to the nearest village for some help. There would have been a doctor in the village. But that was two miles away, and I had little hope that my car would get that far given the amount of snow there was on the road. There was little doubt that my only course of action was to look after the boy myself.

I tried to speak to him, but I got no response. It was almost as if he was hynotised, with his eyes just staring straight ahead, and he didn't seem to know that I was there.

I turned up the heating in the house. I didn't really care if it was going to be unbearably hot for me, but I needed to get his body temperature up. That was about all I knew when it came to what I thought could be hypothermia. I went upstairs and took the quilt from the bed and brought it downstairs, but it was no use covering him with it if he was lying there in wet clothes. I felt bad doing it, but I took off his clothes, and dressed him in a pair of my own pyjamas before covering him with the quilt and drying his hair with a towel.

"What were you doing out there?" I asked.

I didn't expect a response, and I didn't get one.

"What's your name?" I asked him.

Again, there was no response, but my efforts were to try and bring him around from whatever trance-like state he was in. I went into the kitchen to make some tea, thinking a hot drink would help to warm him up. I checked on him every now and then while I did so. There seemed no improvement in him until I brought the cup of tea up to his lips and he almost instinctively took a sip, and his eyes looked into mine. I started to believe that I might make progress after all. I didn't get him to drink all of the tea, but at least he had some of it.

I confess that I was somewhat curious as to who he might be, and so I went through his trouser pockets in search of some identification. I found a set of keys and a couple of tissues in the front pockets, and a wallet in the back one. Upon opening it, I came across a driver's license that informed me that the young man on my sofa was Benjamin Haydn and that he was nineteen years old. I put the wallet back into the pocket and walked back over to him, kneeling down on the floor beside him.

"Benjamin?" I asked, hoping that there might be some sense of recognition to his name, but I detected none.

I was still unsure what to do with him, but with no working phone or internet, and the snow too deep for me to transport him either home or to a doctor, I decided the best thing that I could do was to simply keep him as warm and comfortable as I could. Bearing this in mind, I took him off the sofa, carried him upstairs, and put him down on my bed, covering him up with the quilt. I didn't know what else to do, and this action seemed the most sensible.

I went back downstairs, and switched on the television. There wasn't much of a reception. There was a signal one minute but not the next, but I did manage to catch a few moments of the news, which usefully told me about the heavy snowfall that I was already very aware of. There was an emergency number to use, but that wasn't exactly helpful given that the phones weren't working.

I decided that the best thing I could do was to kill some time by writing up some of my monograph while we still had electricity. I went back upstairs and sat down at the laptop and switched it on. While it booted up, I gazed out of the window at the rather splendid view. The snow had stopped falling – at least, for the time being – and it made it easier to see how great the snowfall had been overnight, as well as how cut off the cottage was.

The window of the bedroom I was using as my office faced the back garden, and I wondered, perhaps for the first time, just why that large expanse of land hadn't been built on since the fire that had destroyed the old school. I was sure that the letting agent had told me that the fire had happened some fifty years ago. It seemed odd such a prime piece of land remained unused. It officially came with the cottage, but clearly no-one had made any attempt at using it as a garden. It was just a mess of overgrown weeds on the other side of the small fence that once had marked the territorial boundaries of the cottage.

Once the laptop had started up, I tried to concentrate on my work, while checking on my guest every hour or so. I got a surprising amount of work done. The house was deathly quiet – I didn't put music on for fear of waking up Benjamin – and no vehicle came past the cottage due to the snow. I assumed that a snow plough would reach me eventually, but I feared it might be a day or two away. I was just thankful that we still had electricity.

After typing up four or five pages – almost a record for me in the given time frame – I went downstairs to make myself another drink and to try to come up with something that I fancied to eat. I thought I would probably make do with a tin of soup, and use up some of the bread that I had brought with me the day before.

It was as I was standing at the fridge that I heard footsteps from upstairs, which eventually made their way down the staircase. I went into the living room to find Benjamin standing at the bottom of the stairs. I smiled at him, in an attempt to be as unthreatening as I could possibly be.

"Hello," I said.

My guest looked at me, but seemed confused.

"Where am I?" he asked.

"You're at a cottage about two miles from the village," I told him. "I found you outside in the snow this morning."

"Why was I out there?"

"I don't know," I said. "I'm sorry. A policeman came here last night and pretty much told me to expect you."

"He told you that I would come here?" Benjamin asked, understandably bewildered.

"Not you, specifically. Just someone. A young man, he said. He told me that this happened quite regularly when there was this kind of weather in the area."

At this comment, there seemed to be some kind of recognition in his face.

"So, this is the old school cottage?" he asked.

I nodded.

"Yes," I said. "How do you know?"

He looked as if he was feeling faint, and he grabbed hold of the banister at the bottom of the stairs.

"Why don't you sit down?" I said, and guided him into a chair, which he almost collapsed into. "Would you like something to eat or drink? Something hot? Tea or coffee, perhaps?"

"Tea would be nice, thank you," Benjamin said.

"Anything to eat?" I asked him.

He thought for a moment, not quite sure.

"I was going to have some tomato soup," I said to him. "Would you like some of that?"

Benjamin nodded his head.

"Yes. Thank you."

"I'm Paul," I said to him, as I went back into the kitchen.

"I'm Benjamin," he said.

"Yes, I know. I found your wallet. I would have informed the police or got you a doctor, but all the phones are out. And my car wouldn't get through the snow. So, I'm afraid you're stuck with my company for a few days, possibly."

He smiled at me.

"I'm sorry for the inconvenience of having me here," Benjamin said.

"It's fine," I told him. "I'm just glad you are OK. You didn't even have a coat."

I handed him his cup of tea.

"Thank you," he said. "They never have a coat."

"They?"

"The people who are found here at the cottage. I guess I'm just lucky that you were living here and saw me. A few years ago, this happened and the boy died."

"So, you know what all of this is about?" I asked.

"Yes. All of the villagers know about it. But sometimes when this happens, it's kept quieter than others."

"Why?"

"It's a long story," Benjamin said.

We agreed that he would tell me the story after we

had eaten.

Benjamin said that he wasn't particularly hungry, and yet he ate his soup quickly. I asked him how he was feeling, and he said he was tired, but otherwise he felt OK.

"You're lucky," I said. "I really didn't know that you were going to get better without proper treatment when I came across you this morning, but I'm guessing that you hadn't been out there as long as I first thought."

"I don't remember anything about it," he said. "I remember getting out of bed at some point last night, and then waking up in your bed an hour or so ago. I don't remember anything else about it. Perhaps it's for the best."

I agreed with him. He sat there in silence for a few seconds, and then he took a deep breath and began his story.

"It's all to do with the school that was here," he said. "Nobody really remembers it in the village. It closed down just before the start of the Second World War, and so anyone still around would only have been young children back then. I guess someone in their nineties might have a memory of it, but there's only one person of that age in the village that I can think of, and she doesn't have much memory of anything."

"Why did it close down?" I asked.

"There was something of a scandal. I guess that's what you'd call it. The man who ran the school was known in the village for being something of a tyrant."

"He didn't treat the kids well?"

Benjamin nodded.

"Something like that. But he didn't treat the teachers well, either. Or anyone else who worked at the school. Stories spread about him in the village. They still do, but I don't know how many of them are true and how many are gossip."

"That's always the case," I agreed.

"There were a couple of young people about my age working there, so the story goes. They had been pupils there, and they stayed on there to help out. Probably looking after the building or something."

"Maybe even some teaching," I told him. "There were less regulations back then."

"They lived at the school," Benjamin said. "That's what I've been told, anyway. It was the middle of winter, and the weather was like this. The headmaster of the school went to find them late one night. Nobody really knows what he wanted – it was probably just to speak to them about keeping the school warm or something like that. But the story says that he found them together. In bed, presumably. He went mad, and sent them outside into the snow as a punishment, and made them stay there. Just in whatever they were wearing. No hat or coat or boots or anything. He made them stand in the grounds all night and into the next day. It was only when one of them collapsed that the other teachers got together and went against the headmaster. The boys were brought in, but one of them died. The headmaster was removed from the post, but I don't know if he was charged with any crime. The school closed down shortly after."

It was a horrible story, but I had little doubt that it was true.

"And now," I said, "whenever there's the same kind of weather, a boy from the village finds himself re-enacting what happened to the two young men back then?"

Benjamin nodded.

"Yes. Not just any boy of the same age. It's only those that are gay. That's why there have been times when it has been hushed up. There were always stories that these things happened, but often the people involved didn't want it known. Being gay in a village is still not always easy once people find out and the gossip starts."

"And what about the school burning down? Do you know anything about that?"

"Possibly. It's said that a boy died of hypothermia after being drawn to the school and standing outside in a blizzard, and that his mother or father came here in a rage and set fire to the main school building. It's only a rumour, though. Village gossip."

I sat there quietly, trying to take in the story that I had been told. I had never been a believer of ghosts and the supernatural, but there must have been something in the tale for it to have been kept alive for eighty years – and for the local policeman to have come and warned me the previous evening.

"People in the village know that I'm gay," Benjamin said, as if he was reading my thoughts. "I reckon that's why Harry came to see you."

"Harry?"

"The policeman in the village. He would know that I was gay and the right age, and that I could end up here considering the weather."

"You told me that one of the people who ended up here died?" I said.

"Yes," Benjamin said. "That last happened five or six years ago. Maybe a bit longer. There was no-one in the cottage then. Nobody's lived in it for many years, but the owner died, and his family has decided to let it. You're the first person to live here for many years. Lucky for me that you were here. I could be dead, otherwise."

*

It was another three days before the snow stopped falling completely and the snow plough reached us. Luckily, the phone signal had returned prior to that and so Benjamin had been able to call his parents and tell them that he was safe. He did a very good job of staying quiet during the day while I did some work, and then we ate dinner in the evenings and watched a film on the television.

When I took him home, his mother was overcome with emotion, and didn't stop thanking me for my efforts during the time I was there. She tried to get me to stay to dinner, but I told her I needed to be getting back to Susan and the kids. The incident in the cottage had made me feel as if I wanted to see them at the earliest opportunity – and I felt guilty for sometimes thinking of them as a distraction to my work.

Before I left the village to go home, I stopped off at the small police station in the village, and thanked Harry, the constable, for having called on me during my first night in the cottage, in order to prepare me for what happened.

"Think nothing of it," he said. "I am just sorry that I didn't think I could tell you the whole story at the time. But I was worried you'd think I was barking mad."

"Well, you probably saved young Benjamin's life by coming to see me," I told him.

"Well, at least something came out of the visit. But you can only do so much, and I feel so bad about Martin. His parents are distraught."

I was confused.

"Martin?" I asked. "Who is Martin?"

"Why, he's Benjamin's young man, Sir. He went missing from the village on the same night, but nobody has seen or heard from him since. I have to break that news to young Benjamin, now that he is home. I didn't feel it was right to tell him on the phone when he called us from the cottage to say that he was fine. In all honesty, I have a horrible feeling that we won't find Martin until the snow has melted."

I wondered if I could have helped Benjamin's boyfriend, too, if I had only looked out for him.

When I returned to the cottage in the new year, I learned that Martin still hadn't been found, even after the cold spell had ended. Benjamin told me that he was hoping that his boyfriend had simply run away, but neither of us really believed that to be the case.

THE GIFT

Once upon a time, not so long ago (quite recently, actually), an old man took his niece to see Father Christmas in his grotto in a department store.

The niece was, by this point, eight years old, and the man knew that this would be the last year that she would be interested in going to see the man dressed all in red with the long white beard. Children were not innocent for as long as they used to be. In fact, the man was surprised that she still believed that Santa existed, and even wondered if she just wanted to go in order to get a free present from the visit.

He hoped that he was just being cynical – he had been more cynical lately.

The queue was quite long to see Father Christmas, but not as long as it had been in previous years. Another sign that even the great traditions start to die out eventually. Perhaps it was more difficult to believe in Father Christmas after close to two years of a pandemic. Most of the people waiting in the queue were wearing masks, which the old man was thankful for. He wondered if some people would wear them permanently, now. And, when they finally entered Father Christmas's little grotto (there had clearly been budget cuts), they saw that he was wearing one, too – even if it didn't fit particularly well due to his beard.

The old man watched as his niece went and sat on a chair beside Father Christmas, and looked up at his face. He assumed that she was scrutinizing the man in front of her. Was the beard real? Were his cheeks really that red? How old was this Father Christmas? Maybe forty at most. He most certainly was just a man in a costume.

Father Christmas asked the girl her name, and how old she was, and she told him. And then he asked her if she had been well behaved all year. The old man smiled as she said:

"We've all had to be well-behaved this year, haven't we?"

"Yes," Father Christmas said. "I suppose we have."

He looked at the girl's uncle and winked at him, as if to say, "you've got a smart one here."

A short chat later, and it was all over. Father Christmas picked one of the presents from the floor beside him, and handed it to the girl. She said thank you, and asked if she would see him again next year.

"Well, I don't know about that," Father Christmas

told her. "There's only so much time, and so many children to see. Perhaps you have had your time of coming to visit me over the last few years. Time to give the little ones a chance, don't you think?"

The girl thought for a moment, and then nodded her head.

"Yes, I guess you are right."

She turned to her uncle and reached for his hand.

"Just wait a moment or two," Father Christmas said to the girl. "Why don't you wait outside for a couple of minutes, while I talk to your uncle here? I think he might need a present from me, too."

The girl nodded, and went outside.

"How did you know I was her uncle?" the old man asked.

"I know lots of things," Father Christmas said.

"But I was much more likely to be her grandfather."

"Yes, you were. But you're not. And Father Christmas knows more than you could possibly imagine."

The old man smiled.

"You speak as if I don't know that you are just a man in a suit and a false beard," he said.

"And how do you know that I am?"

"I'm seventy-five," the man said. "Not seven."

"Does that matter?" Father Christmas asked him. "I've been around for hundreds of years. You know that. Where do you think all of those stories come from? There's no smoke without fire, you know?"

The old man was bemused, and a little unnerved.

"I should go and make sure my niece is alright," he said.

"She's just fine," Father Christmas said to him. "Now, why don't you tell me what *you* would like most for Christmas? You look to me as if you are rather sad. As if you need something to restore your faith – not in a God or some religion, but your faith in life. You *are* sad, are you not?"

The old man nodded.

"Yes," he said. "I guess I don't hide it very well."

"Nobody hides sadness very well. And grief is even harder to mask. You *are* grieving, aren't you?"

"I lost someone close to me," the old man said, his eyes tearing up.

"Someone very close, I think?" Father Christmas asked him.

"My husband."

"Then, if you don't mind me saying, you didn't just lose someone close to you, you lost part of yourself."

The old man felt tears welling up in his eyes.

"Yes. Yes, I suppose I did."

"Had you been married long?"

"As long as it has been legal."

"And before that?"

"We had been together forty years. He passed away forty years ago to the day after I first met him. He was my life. And, I suppose, I was his. I'm sorry, I shouldn't be taking up your time."

Father Christmas smiled at him.

"It is difficult to take up much of my time when I

have as much of it as I do. What's a few minutes in hundreds of years?"

"I wish we had had hundreds of years together," the old man said, a tear slowly rolling down his cheek.

"Some would try to tell you that you *will* have hundreds of years together in the future."

"I don't believe," the old man said. "I did once. When I was a kid. But not anymore. I can't believe in a God that brings so much misery to the world. Who took my husband away from me."

"He had been ill for some time?"

The old man nodded.

"Yes. But just because you know that something is coming, that it's inevitable, it doesn't make it any easier. He was already weak, and, as soon as he got the virus, it was only ever going to end one way."

"I'm sorry to hear that."

The man wiped a tear from his cheek.

"Thank you for listening," he said. "But I should let you get on with your work. You have a long queue outside."

The old man took a final look at Father Christmas, still somewhat confused by the conversation, and then walked towards the grotto door.

"Mr. Sullivan," Father Christmas said.

The old man stopped and turned around to face him. He had not told Father Christmas his name.

"You are Arnold Sullivan, are you not?"

The old man nodded.

"How did you know that?"

"I know lots more than you could possibly imagine," Father Christmas said. "And coming up with your name is, I'm afraid, little more than a parlour trick. Something to get your attention. You might not believe in any religion, but I would like to think that you might at least believe in *me*. You did once, after all."

"That was many years ago."

The two men looked at each other, and Arnold Sullivan felt something happening to him. He felt a kind of warmth enter his body, and it radiated through his chest, up into his head, and down his arms and legs.

"*Do* you believe in me now?" Father Christmas asked him.

Arnold Sullivan said that he did, although he wasn't sure why. This was, surely, a man in a Santa suit who simply happened to be able to read people well. Just like a mind-reader at a fair.

"I cannot bring the love of your life back to you," Father Christmas said. "I cannot raise the dead. I only wish I could. But there is one gift that I *can* give you. I will give you the gift of knowing that your loved one will always be with you."

Arnold would normally have said that such a thing couldn't happen, but something stopped him. "Believe in me," Father Christmas had said.

Arnold nodded his head.

"Thank you," he said, and walked out of the grotto.

Arnold Sullivan found his niece in the toy department of the department store, and she asked him what he had said to Father Christmas after she had left.

THE GIFT

He told her that they just wished each other a Merry Christmas, and then he suggested that they go and get some lunch.

A few hours later, he took his niece back to her parents, and had dinner with them. They asked him how the day had gone, and he said he had thoroughly enjoyed himself. They kept asking him if he was alright, saying that he seemed distant. Arnold told them that he was just tired, and that he wasn't as young as he used to be.

When he got home, it was to a quiet and empty cottage – the cottage that he and his husband had bought together many years earlier. The home they were to spend their old age together in. Arnold had thought about selling it. He wasn't sure that he could carry on living in the house that was so full of memories of his husband. At the same time, he wasn't sure he could leave those memories, either.

Arnold made himself a cup of tea and took it upstairs to bed, where he read for about half an hour and then switched off the light. He thought he would be unable to sleep, that the strange conversation with the department store Santa would keep whirring around in his mind for hours, and yet he fell asleep quicker than usual.

When he awoke, it was two o'clock in the morning. It wasn't like him to wake up in the middle of the night, and, at first, he wondered why he had done so. He had been dreaming. Only remnants of it remained, but Jacob, Arnold's husband, had been in the dream. He was sure of that. But the more he tried to remember the dream, the more the details of it slipped away from him. He decided he would get out of bed, go to the bathroom, and then get himself a hot drink. Perhaps some Horlicks, if the packet that he had in the cupboard wasn't past its use-by date. He reached over to the bedside lamp and switched it on. Standing at the end of the bed, dressed in a dinner suit with a bright red bow-tie, was Jacob.

Arnold shut his eyes and then opened them again, thinking that the apparition was a small leftover vision from the dream that he had just woken from. But when he opened his eyes again, Jacob was still there, smiling at him. He didn't look ghostly, other than having a kind of aura around him – a light shadow, almost, like you would have seen on an old television set that wasn't quite tuned in to its channel properly. Jacob didn't look well, and neither had he done so in life. His health had been deteriorating for years prior to his death. And yet, despite that, he looked handsome in his dinner suit. He always did. Perhaps that was why he was wearing it now.

Arnold sat up in bed, trying to understand what he was seeing.

"Jacob?" he said, quietly. "Is that you?"

Jacob nodded his head slowly.

"Yes," he said. "It's me. I would under normal circumstances say, 'in the flesh,' but that's not strictly true on this occasion."

"Always the one with the joke," Arnold said.

THE GIFT

"That's me," Jacob confirmed. "Are you pleased to see me?"

Arnold slowly pushed back the duvet, and got out of bed.

"Pleased to see you?" he said. "I would give anything for this not to be a dream."

"It's not a dream. It may feel like one. And you might think it's one when you get up in the morning, but this is really happening."

"But how?"

"How?" Jacob sounded incredulous. "Father Christmas, of course."

"Now I know you're joking."

Jacob shook his head.

"Far from it. True, it's not very often that he grants these kinds of wishes. But you would be surprised at how many letters get sent to him from what you might call 'older children.' People *our* age. And they ask for all kinds of things, but most of them can't be bought like the children's presents. But he saw you this afternoon with little Josephine – not so little these days, though, is she? How old is she now?"

"Eight."

"She'll stop believing in the man in the red suit soon – if she hasn't already. But then, when people get to our age – well, *your* age – people don't so much believe in him as to hope he's real. They need hope. And Father Christmas today saw that you needed *something* to give you hope. And here I am. For one night only, as they say."

Arnold didn't quite know what to do. He knew it couldn't be happening, despite how much Jacob was trying to convince him.

"Can I...can I touch you?" he asked.

Jacob opened his arms.

"I'm your husband," he said. "Of course, you can touch me. Come."

Arnold moved slowly around the bed so that he was just a few inches away from Jacob. He paused for a moment or two, and then stepped forward into the arms that were waiting to hold him. He buried his head into his husband's chest.

"Jacob! I have missed you so much," he said, tears streaming down his face. "Why did you have to leave me?"

"My time had come. Clichéd, I know. But true. It happens to us all. It has happened to too many over the last year or so."

Arnold didn't reply. Instead, the two men stood there, embracing, just as they had done for forty years. And then, slowly, Arnold reached up to the face of his husband and caressed it. That felt real, too.

"Can I?" he asked. "Is that allowed?"

"You can do what you want," Jacob told him.

"I want to kiss you."

"Then kiss me, Arnold."

When the lips of the two men met a second or two later, it was as if time had stood still. The love between them was the same as it had been four decades earlier. Jacob's lips felt the same as they had back then, when they had kissed for the first time while walking home from the cinema. Times had been different then. They had to make sure that they weren't seen when they were holding hands or hugging or kissing. And there had been no Coronavirus, of course, but there had been another threat that would arrive in the country just a matter of months later, and which would take many of their friends in the most horrible of ways.

"How long can you stay?" Arnold asked.

"Not long."

"I feared you would say that."

"You were told this afternoon that Father Christmas cannot raise the dead, but that he could make sure you know that I will always be with you. I *will* always be here," Jacob said. "Even at times when you feel utterly despondent and life is bleak, I will be here, holding your hand. We never got to say goodbye on the night when I passed on. Perhaps you would know these things already if we had. But believe me when I tell you that, when you cry, I shall reach out and I shall comfort you. You won't see me, you won't feel me touch you, but you will *know*. I will never ever leave you, my darling."

The strangest thing of this unexpected meeting was that the two men had no idea of how best to use their small amount of time together. Talk seemed so redundant. Love-making would seem wrong. And so it was that the two men lay down on the bed, with Arnold's head resting on Jacob's chest, and his arm holding him close. They didn't speak. They barely moved. They just shared their love of each other through the simple act of a cuddle.

For the first time since Jacob had died, Arnold was at peace, but he knew that, if he eventually fell asleep, Jacob would not be there when he awoke. And yet, of course, the inevitable happened, and Arnold did doze off while holding his love of four decades.

When he awoke, several hours later, the first thing that he did was to look across at the other side of the double bed. He instinctively knew that it was empty, but he had to look just to make sure. It had been a dream, after all, probably sparked by that strange conversation with Father Christmas the previous afternoon.

Utterly devastated, Arnold got out of bed, put his feet into his slippers, and wrapped his dressing gown around him. He slowly walked down the stairs and into the kitchen to switch the kettle on to make himself some tea.

Propped up against the kettle was a Christmas card, which had not been there night before. Arnold picked it up and opened the envelope. The front of the card had a picture of Father Christmas in his grotto, talking to a child. Arnold opened the card. Inside was shaky handwriting that he recognised at once. It read as follows:

To Arnold,
I love you with all of my heart, and remember that, despite the fact you can no longer see me, I shall always

be by your side.
>
> Lots of love, my darling.
>
> Jacob.
>
> xxx"

Arnold cried. He had no real notion of whether they were tears of joy or of sadness. He looked at the card, knowing that there was no real explanation as to how it got there, or how it had Jacob's handwriting in it. After some minutes of crying and trying to pull himself together, Arnold took the card into the living room and stood it on the mantelpiece. Then he picked up his mug from the coffee table, and took it through into the kitchen. Beside the kettle now was the red bow-tie that Jacob had worn just a few hours earlier.

Later that day, Arnold decided that he would return to see Father Christmas in his grotto at the department store, in order to thank him for what he had said and done. But the grotto wasn't there. When he asked a shop assistant what had happened to it, he was told that there had been no grotto this year, mostly due to concerns over social distancing and a lack of ventilation in what was a small space. Arnold thanked him for his time and slowly walked home.

A NOTE FROM THE AUTHOR

Four of the five stories in this volume were written over a very short space of time in November 2021. The exception, *Breaking Up is Hard to Do* was written for a *Hallowed Histories* podcast in the autumn of 2020.

The reason for the writing of the four new stories was that I wanted a short break from writing my new horror novel called *Marlington,* which will be published in Spring 2022, and I thought a small group of short ghost stories for Christmas might well be a fun diversion.

However, they might have been written in a relatively short space of time, but the ideas for them come from a much longer period. For example, the final story (the only one that is not a horror tale) is based on something I wrote around the age of fifteen – and that, my friends, was a very long time ago! I always thought

I would return to it at some point, and it fitted quite nicely as a kind of heartwarming coda to this slim volume.

Meanwhile, a village called Brandley appears in two of the other stories, and it is very much based on a real Norfolk village (but here I have given it a different name). And the cottage that takes centre stage in *Houses Never Forget* is very real (and still standing), and used to frighten me every time I walked (sorry, ran) past it as a child.

As I have already mentioned, a new horror novel called *Marlington* will be published at some point in the spring of 2022, and there is a plan for a new Michael & Peter book that will, hopefully, appear at the end of the same year. I've received some very nice comments about the previous two books in the series (*The Pied Piper* and *The School Bell*), and I hope to revisit those characters on a regular basis.

Thank you for supporting this little book of ghost stories, and, as the famous poem concludes:

Happy Christmas to all, and to all a good night!

Printed in Great Britain
by Amazon